BLOODY MONDAY . . .

The Executioner was going out with a bang, not a sigh. . . .

"The job isn't finished. The wiseguys are just lying low, waiting for the heat to subside. I know who they are and where they are. They'll be popping up again, stronger than ever. I can't give them that."

"You can give them your last chance for a real life, though, can't you?" Brognola replied bitterly. "What can you do with one lousy week?"

"I can give it a proper mop-up."

"Where?"

"Everywhere. A quick blitz in each major region of the country. I count six of those. Give me some air support and I'll do it in six days."

Six days, sure. Mind-boggling. If the guy could survive them, Mack Bolan would thereafter abruptly cease to exist, in any legal sense, and the Phoenix Project would arise from the ashes of that lost identity.

The final days . . . a second long mile through Hell . . . and already the sun had arisen on Monday . . . bloody Monday.

The Executioner Series:

the EXECUTIONER

#33

MONDAY'S MOB
by Don Pendleton

PINNACLE BOOKS   •   NEW YORK

EXECUTIONER #33: MONDAY'S MOB

Copyright © 1978 by Don Pendleton

All rights reserved, including the right to reproduce this book or portions thereof in any form.

An original Pinnacle Books edition, published for the first time anywhere.

First printing, October 1978
Second printing, September 1979
Third printing, June 1980
Fourth printing, November 1981

ISBN: 0-523-41815-9

Cover illustration by Gil Cohen

Printed in the United States of America

PINNACLE BOOKS, INC.
1430 Broadway
New York, New York 10018

For all the nice folk of
the heartland—or spell
that *hearthland*—with
due apologies for whatever
liberties have been taken herein
with your blessed countenance.

dp

"And whosoever shall compel thee
to go a mile,
Go with him twain."
—Sermon on the Mount

"Like one that on a lonesome road
Doth walk in fear and dread,
And having once turned round walks on,
And turns no more his head;
Because he knows a frightened fiend
Doth close behind him tread."
—Coleridge (The Ancient Mariner)

"Brognola says I've done my mile
in Hell. So okay, let's start
the second mile.
But let's not look back."
—Mack Bolan, from his Journal

MONDAY'S MOB

PROLOGUE

Mack Bolan's personal war against the Mafia had erupted as a spontaneous reaction to a terrible injustice. The young sergeant from Vietnam had not even known the true pedigree of this new enemy at home when he opened the ceremonies on a Pittsfield street with five blasts from a sniper's rifle; he knew only that they were legal untouchables, that they were responsible for the destruction of his family, that there could be no point to his own life without some answer to the atrocity.

Bolan had an answer. He had already become a quiet legend in the hellgrounds of Southeast Asia where his expertise as a deathmaster had earned him the label, "The Executioner." He had been officially credited with nearly a hundred kills of enemy VIPs when the tragedy at home recalled him from the second combat tour. And, yes, the Executioner had an answer for the tragedy on the home front. He brought that answer from the steamy jungles of Vietnam and deposited it on the quiet streets of his home town.

And then the awful truth came down. *Mafia!* And Mack Bolan knew, then, that he had another unwinnable war by the tail. A sympathetic homicide cop unofficially urged the young soldier to return quickly to that other war zone, where his chances for survival would be infinitely better. There was no point, now, to his remaining in Pittsfield. He had secured his "pound of flesh" and forced a balance on the scales of justice; nothing but his own certain death could possibly await him here.

But Mack Bolan had other ideas. And he had come into a new truth. He knew now that the greatest enemy the American nation could contemplate was that enemy within—that cancerous, scabrous, vile growth on the nation's innards—that power that knowing federal officials had characterized as "the second invisible government of the nations"—the Mafia, La Cosa Nostra, the Mob, the Outfit, the Organization; by whatever name, it was the new enemy and Mack Bolan could not turn his back upon it.

Instead, he brought war to it.

Quite to his own surprise, he survived the ensuing battle for Pittsfield—and it was a resounding victory for the one-man army. He knew, however, that he had won a minor skirmish, not a war. And he knew that this new

2

enemy was virtually infinite in terms of power and resources. But they were not gods. They had weaknesses that could be exploited by a savvy soldier. Still, as he faded from the scene of that initial engagement, Bolan felt that his own days were. definitely numbered—measurable perhaps as a given number of heartbeats. In his own understanding, he had embarked upon his "bloody last mile," determined only to "eat their bowels as they ingest me."

As it turned out, that last mile was rather elastic. It stretched across more than thirty pitched battles and onto several continents as this remarkable warrior grew into his destiny and transcended the most hallowed concepts of duty and valor. He became far more than just a soldier—as he preferred to think of himself. Mack Bolan became a force in the world—a thundering angel, as it were—a heartening and inspiring model for individual commitment and high achievement, a spur and a goad to law enforcement agencies everywhere, a chilling wind and justification for pervading paranoia within the organized underworld. The marksman's medal was his dreaded calling card; a wispy shadow in combat black his shivery presence; flames of war and pyramiding attrition his jolting effect on the "omnipotent" enemy. More devastating than all, perhaps, was his ability to walk among them as one of the flock, to sit down with them at their councils, to drink their wine and break their bread—even to command them, and divide them, and pit faction against faction so that they may eat themselves.

It was quite a mile, yes.

He had been hounded and pursued by the law and the lawless alike—the most wanted criminal of all, in the law's blind stare; the most threatening and demoralizing enemy of all, in the Mob's fevered gaze. Yet wherever he halted and planted his feet for the stand or for the counterattack, the vaunted enemy fell writhing while the law—those soldiers of the same side—watched in awe and admiration.

Mack Bolan's war was not with the law but with those who confounded the law. And he did not make war on the badge, not even a tarnished one. The hand of friendship or the salute of respect was always there for any badge that would accept it, however grudgingly; consequently, Mack Bolan's last mile had attracted warm friendships and clandestine allies from various levels of the police community.

Early in the war, a high official within the U.S. Justice Department had approached the warrior with an offer of amnesty and honors if only he would join the official war against crime. Bolan declined the offer, feeling that he would be severely limited and perhaps totally neutralized by a government sponsorship. That high official was one Harold Brognola, later to become the No. 1 cop in the country, advisor to presidents, NSC expert on domestic subversion. Except for one aberration, Brognola had been Mack Bolan's staunchest champion and most powerful ally within the police community—unofficially, of course. There were others —many others. The closest friend and perhaps most valuable ally was a man whom Bolan had been sworn to execute during the initial struggle at Pittsfield: Leo Turrin, Mafia underboss with the "girls franchise" in western Massachusetts, blood nephew to Sergio Frenchi, the boss of the Berkshires. But Bolan had learned just in time that "Leo the Pussy" was an undercover federal agent—thus, a soldier of the same side who quickly became a total convert to the Bolan cause and an invaluable insider whose counsel and assistance did much to stretch that last impossible mile into an infinite circle.

Other friends had checked in from both sides of the spectrum, as well as from the netural zone of uninvolved bystanders—a tribute to the basic humanity of man and a testament to Bolan's own warn humanity. This lonely warrior was not all death machine. He was a man, as well—one who could inspire fierce loyalties, undying love, towering respect. Through it all, however, he was essentially and necessarily alone. He involved others in his cause with the greatest reluctance and at a stringently minimum level; yet he leapt quickly and decisively to the aid of those in need, without thought for his own jeopardy.

Quite a mile, yes.

But now it appeared to have found its natural end.

Unable to withstand the repeated onslaughts of Bolan's raging brand of warfare and falling apart under its own attrition at the top, the once invincible Organization was now scattered into fearful bands of huddled paranoiacs, distrustful of one another yet loath to walk alone the twisted roads of their own hellgrounds.

Bolan had been carefully reading all the signs and he knew what was happening in Mafiadom. Others, also, were keeping abreast of the situation. Harold Brognola had journeyed to Nashville where he held a secret parley with Bolan following an operation there, and where he not only confirmed "the imminent dissolution of organized crime in America" but also brought to Bolan an offer that most men would find impossible to refuse.

The President had created a sensitive new security section, to deal with terrorists and other paramilitary threats to the national security. The man who headed that section would be virtually autonomous, reporting directly to the President himself. The only man for that job was Mack Bolan—that was a consensus decision from Washington.

"It's the same war," Brognola had told his friend the blitz artist, "the same kind of enemy. You haven't been fighting *people*, you know. You've been fighting a *condition*."

Yes, Bolan had known that. And he had been strongly aware of the ugly mood of terrorism sweeping across the western world, already beginning to spill onto the American continent. The need for an effective counterforce was real—and urgent.

Bolan felt that he understood the terrorist mentality, that he could be effective in dealing with it. He had directly experienced the savage effect of terrorist activity on civilian populaces in Southeast Asia—and he agreed with Brognola that western society was in grave peril unless decisive action was immediately taken to discourage the spread of barbarism.

But he was not entirely convinced that the Mafia menace had been sufficiently weakened—that his vow to "shake their house down" had been fulfilled.

The offer from Washington was like a hand from heaven, sure. It included total amnesty and forgiveness, a whole new identity, honors and official status, the full resources of the mightiest nation on earth in close support—a reprieve and a restart, a new life, a new challenge, a new hope.

Above all else, though—an end to that damnable last mile.

The President of the United States had, yeah, made Mack Bolan an offer which could not be refused.

But it was also one which he could not possibly accept; not yet.

At a second meeting with Brognola—in Louisville, twenty-four hours later—Bolan set forth the conditions of his acceptance. And though Brognola huffed and puffed throughout the discussion, he knew from the beginning that no argument was possible. The guy had that look in his eyes, a suggestion of ice just below the surface, and the head fed knew that the big guy simply had to travel that extra mile.

"He's in, sir," Brognola would report to the President, several hours following the meeting in Louisville. "But not for another week. It's a question of ethics, I guess. The second mile syndrome."

"The what?"

"A final walk through hell. I guess he's taking a roll call. Wants to make sure nobody's missing. Then he'll be in. I have his word on that. He *will* be in."

"Or dead," the President replied with a quiet sigh. A moment later he pinned his top internal security advisor with a steely gaze while softly commanding, "He's to have full support on this final walk, whatever that means. I don't want to know the details. I just want you to produce the man in this office, alive and well, one week from right now."

Brognola dropped his eyes with embarrassment as he responded to that. "There are, uh, extra-legal overtones to, uh—"

"I said I don't want to know the details, Hal."

It was just as well. There was very little Brognola could offer, anyway, in the nature of full support. Bolan would not tolerate any direct intervention. His only request had been for a C-130 transport—air logistics support.

As for those details—nobody would have believed them, anyway. Even Brognola, knowing the guy as he did, had found the whole thing just a bit mind-boggling.

8

The Executioner was going out with a bang, not a sigh. That second mile would be as elastic as the first—though greatly compressed in time.

Six days.

The guy had asked for six lousy days. "I'll need another week, Hal."

"For what?"

"The job isn't finished. The wise guys are just lying low, waiting for the heat to subside. I know who they are and where they are. They'll be popping up again, stronger than ever. I can't give them that."

"You can give them your last chance for a real life, though, can't you?" Brognola replied bitterly. "What can you do with one lousy week?"

"I can give it a proper mop-up."

"Where?"

"Everywhere. A quick blitz in each major region of the country. I count six of those. Give me some air support and I'll do it in six days."

Six days, sure. Mind-boggling. The final days of the Executioner. If the guy could survive them, Mack Bolan would thereafter abruptly cease to exist, in any legal sense, and the Phoenix Project would arise from the ashes of that lost identity.

Six days, the final days—a second long mile through Hell . . . and already the sun had arisen on Monday, bloody Monday.

CHAPTER 1

THE MARK

The crosshairs of the sniperscope were centered on the hood ornament of a gleaming Cadillac El Dorado. A dozen or so other luxury cars surrounded the El Dorado, including several more Cadillacs in varied styles, a Mercedes, a couple of Continentals.

Pulled up in front and probably awaiting a load was an empty semitrailer transporter.

A large metal building in the near background was the recycling center for the largest stolen car operation west of New York. This one happened to be nestled in the gentle hills of northwest Kentucky, just outside Louisville.

The tall man in black with the cool eye at the scope had watched as six "refurbished" vehicles rolled from the building to the loading yard during the past hour alone. It did not require a math whiz to compute the value of that one-hour production at somewhere around a hundred thousand dollars. Judging from the size of the building in which the refurbishing was taking place, the twenty-four-hour operation could easily produce six cars per hour right around the clock.

There had not been time to fully scout the operation but the pre-intelligence suggested a typical major recycle. Freelancers would bring in the stolen product—probably most of it from the surrounding states of Indiana, Missouri, Tennessee, Ohio, West Virginia—for something like ten cents on the dollar, market value, maybe a bit more for highly favored models. Night deliveries, probably. The standard plant time for each vehicle would average no more than a few hours for cleaning, touchup paint, a general cosmetic renewal, new serial numbers and counterfeit paperwork.

Bolan had been hearing rumors about this particular "plant" for months and had stumbled onto some fresh input while in Tennessee. Wholesalers Car Refinishers, Inc. was fronted by one Benjamin Davis, a "legitimate" businessman of Louisville. Real owner: Carmine Tuscanotte's Underwriters' Salvage Services, Inc.—an Illinois firm that came under the larger umbrella of North American Investment Services Corporation, which was owned jointly by Tuscanotte and Chicago hood James "Jimmy the Jump" Altorise. Included under that umbrella were a score or more of closely related enterprises such as used car dealerships in more than a dozen states, finance companies, collection agencies, auto wholesalers and transporters, a couple of auction yards.

It was a sweet setup, yeah, and the illicit profits astronomical. The up-front losers were, of course, the nation's insurance companies. Perhaps many people would shed no tears over that. But insurance companies never lose. The ultimate loser was the American motoring public—for whom the insurance premiums kept soaring higher and higher.

Bolan knew that organized auto theft was milking billions each year from the U.S. economy—and that was concern enough, right there, of course—but his interest of the moment was not with auto theft but with the personalities bankrolling this particular operation. Both Tuscanotte and Altorise had "gone cool" recently, abandoning their usual haunts and submerging from both public and underworld view. The Chicago outfit had been in turmoil for a long time, hardly recovering from Bolan's strike there before being torn by internal strife as inevitably the younger turks began jockeying for the reins of power.

So the enemy had engaged itself in Illinois. Bolan had kept interested tabs on the developments in that area. His recent paralyzing strike on the national headquarters in New York had produced strong secondary effects in the Midwest—perhaps inspiring the rash of gangland hits in and around Chicago as uneasy *Mafiosi* moved to protect their flanks.

There was no doubt whatever that Chicago remained the nerve center for organized crime in the nation's midsection. But the scene there was too chaotic. Bolan's personal feeling was that the real powers remaining behind the Chicago Mob had dispersed themselves to the hinterlands—lying low and cooling it while the street bosses fought it out for control of the petty territories.

This was precisely why Mack Bolan was seated on a hillside in Kentucky, contemplating the probably effect of a quick blow to a multimillion dollar car-theft ring.

He sighed with real regret as he chambered a hefty round into the impressive Weatherby .460 and took a final scan through the scope. The sun was about ten minutes into the sky, behind him. Several hundred feet below and about a quarter-mile away, the overhead door of the building was opening to disgorge another gleamingly "refinished" Cadillac. He found the hood ornament with the crosshairs, then made a calculated adjustment to an imaginary mark beneath that hood as he squeezed into the pull.

The big round tore through polished metal and found vital involvement somewhere thereunder. The car lurched, wheezed, and died directly beneath the overhead door, black smoke immediately puffing out through the grillwork. He gave her a couple more in unhurried search as the driver broke clear and ran for cover deeper inside the building. The third round from the big Weatherby evidently found the desired mark as a small explosion sprung the engine hood and sent flames licking over it.

People were scampering about down there, now, in confusion and panic. One guy had grabbed a fire extinguisher and was trying to get some CO_2 under the hood of the stricken car. Bolan shook his head and sent that silly guy 500 splattering grains from the Weatherby. The big slug tore through the CO_2 cylinder and ripped it from the guy's grasp, inspiring saner thoughts and a quick retreat to the interior.

Flames were beginning to lick the underside of the abandoned car when someone inside the building decided to lower the overhead door. Unfortunately the burning vehicle was in the way; the door had hardly settled onto the roof of the car when her gas tank exploded. The door tumbled from its tracks as the exploding vehicle leapt several yards deeper into the interior of the building, blowing much of her fire into the gasoline-paint-solvent-whatever-laden enclosure.

An immediate chain reaction of explosions marked the effect there as Bolan grinned solemnly and went on with the destruction of the massed vehicles outside.

Round after searing round came down off that hillside in a cooly methodical pattern that soon had every third car in flames, with ensuing firestorms reaching out to envelop the whole yard of expensive automobiles.

The barrel of the Weatherby was too hot to touch when Bolan put her down for an assessment of the strike.

It was enough.

Much more than had been hoped for, actually.

There would be no illicit product yield from this recycling plant today. Indeed, there was no more recycling plant. The whole joint was a roaring inferno, flames leaping spectacularly high through jagged holes in the metal roof, walls bowed and gaping from the intolerable pressures inside. Stunned men in work clothing were crouching in frozen groups at safe distances to watch helplessly as the doomed building devoured itself.

Bolan also watched for a moment, then he retrieved his weapon, turned his back on all that, and strolled to the top of the hill.

A Ford station wagon was parked in the grass there, beside a utility pole. A young woman was perched atop the roof of the wagon, her shapely legs crossed Indian fashion at the ankles, eyes glistening.

"What're you doing up there?" inquired the tall man.

"The view is better," she explained. "Like a ringside seat to the burning of Rome. How'd you do that?"

Bolan ignored the unnecessary question as he stowed the Weatherby. "Did he take it?" he asked the lady.

"Yes, sir, he took it." She detached a small tape recorder from the utility pole and handed the device to Bolan. "He called a number in the 812 area."

"Did the number record?"

"Sure did."

16

Bolan grunted with satisfaction, rewound the tape, and punched the playback. The guy took it, yeah.

"Put him on! Quick!"

"Who's this?"

"It's Ben Davis, dammit! Put him on!"

"He ain't here, Mr. Davis. You sound— maybe you better let me have it. This's Harry."

Frantically, then, *"Harry, we're getting hit!"* ..

Pause; then, *"Whattaya mean you—who— what?"* ..

"I don't know! Somebody's shooting us up! The whole place is going up!" ..

"Is it feds or locals? Because if—"

"It's not a raid, Harry! It's not a damn raid! It's a hit!" ..

Very quickly, then, *"Awright, listen, cool it. Just cool it. Call that deputy and get his ass out there on the double! Save all the stuff you can but get rid of all the paper. Understand me? Burn everything that—"*

"I told you, it's already burning! All of it, everything!" ..

A sudden, inspired thought, then, from 812,

"How much dirty product you got sitting around there, Ben?" ..

"What? I got—what?" ..

"You get in there before the firemen come, dammit! Throw acid on everything that's still dirty! You know what I mean!"

Very tiredly, *"I know what you mean, Harry. Okay, I'll try. But listen, dammit, we're under fire. Those bastards are gunning us down! Must be a hundred of 'em up in the hills over our head! I want some damn—"*

That was the end of the conversation from the Kentucky side. The connection popped and sizzled briefly, then died away completely. The guy at 812 shouted a couple of times into the open line, then hung up muttering.

The girl atop the station wagon beamed brightly at the tall man as she declared, "So that's how you did it. A hundred of you, huh?"

Bolan was rewinding the tape.

"Looks like we're going to Indiana," she observed spritely.

He helped her to the ground. "If that's where 812 is, yeah—that's where we're going."

"It's in central Indiana," the lady informed him. "I mean, the prefix he called. Actually, 812 covers most of the state south of Indianapolis. But that's a Columbus number. Indiana, not Ohio."

Bolan showed her a small smile and said, "Right off the top of your head, huh?"

"Sure. That's what this head is for—isn't it?"

He could think of another use or two for that lovely head. He placed a quick kiss on it and told her, "It's for staying on top of your shoulders, Number One. Remember that. Get in the car."

"We're going to Columbus—right?"

"That's where we're going," he assured the lady.

For damned sure, yeah.

The guy at 812 had to be one Harry "the

18

Apeman" Venturi, chief gunbearer to Carmine Tuscanotte.

And Mack Bolan had not come to the Midwest to make war on automobiles.

He'd come to hang the mark of the beast on Carmine Tuscanotte.

CHAPTER 2

APRIL ROSE

The lady had come with the deal. She'd been
selected to babysit Bolan's warwagon—the
twenty-six-foot GMC motorhome that, beneath
that RV exterior, housed a most formidable
capability for making war—and she was the
one who'd loaded the cruiser aboard the C-130
at an air base in New Mexico for transporta-
tion to Louisville.

Bolan had been forced to leave his big
cruiser behind when he responded to the urgent summons from Tennessee, but he definitely needed it for the planned six-day romp
that would ring down the curtain fully and finally, one way or another, on his war with the
Mafia.

As for the lady—she was something else.
Something *extravagantly* else. The name was,
believe it or not, April Rose. She looked like

20

anything but. A tall girl and very strikingly put together with flaring hips and exploding bosom—dark, silky hair and luminous eyes— she would have been well received onstage at Moulin Rouge. Brognola had described her as a "project technician"—which could mean most anything, in Brognola's world. According to the data sheet, she held a degree in electronics and had done considerable graduate work in solid-state physics.

"The lady has it all together," Brognola assured Bolan. "She can be a lot of comfort and you're a damn fool if you don't utilize her talents to the fullest."

"Just what are her talents?" Bolan had warily inquired.

"She can run that bloodmobile for you, I'll guarantee that. The lady could write the book on that Buck Rogers communications gear you have in there. That's mainly why she was selected. I was afraid to turn just anybody loose with that stuff. But she's a lot more than a babysitter for computers. Believe it."

"What exactly does she do, Hal?" Bolan persisted.

"Electronic spying," the head fed muttered, and apparently intended to leave it there.

Bolan grinned and allowed the matter to rest, knowing Brognola's sensitivity to the subject. And he trusted the guy's judgment when it came to personnel. He'd built the most impressive domestic security force ever to emerge from the Washington bureaucracy—and the most effective.

21

Yeah—Bolan trusted Hal Brognola's judgment.

Until he actually put eyes on the lady. By that time, Brognola was back in Washington and April Rose was comfortably ensconced in the warwagon's command chair.

"You don't like what you see," was the lady's first words to Mack Bolan.

This was not entirely true. Even in a baggy military jumpsuit, the lady was a knockout. "I love what I see," he corrected her. "I just don't like where I'm seeing it."

"Would I look more in place flat on my back between satin sheets?" she inquired saucily.

He gave her the level stare as he replied, "Maybe. Look, I—"

"No need to apologize," she said, smiling. "I'm resigned to the reaction. Anyway, I never lay *flat* on my back."

Bolan could believe that.

But she had not given him much time to think about it.

"I took advantage of the flight time to check out your gear. Where'd you get this stuff? I'd like to meet the person who designed it."

Bolan noted that she did not say the *man* who designed it.

"It's straight from outer space. Many of these designs have never been released to public use. Most of this stuff is classified. Where'd you get it?"

Bolan said, "Look, I think you—"

"Those optic systems—how did they combine laser principles with infrared illuminators?

And this navigation system—you have *terrain* following together with—"

Bolan growled, "Hey, hey."

She smiled nervously and said, "Okay, so I'm showing off. I always do that when I'm scared. You make me nervous when you look at me like that. Stop scowling, will you? Actually, no, I'm—well, yes I am. I'm scared to death. Mr. Brognola told me who you really are, of course. That was necessary. Oh, don't worry, you're *Striker*—that's it, that's all, no questions asked—but really . . . yes I am scared to death."

He said, "Shut it off. Right now."

She shut it off, dropping those great eyes with a resigned swoop toward the floor between them.

He said, "I've been trying to tell you that you're welcome aboard. The fault is entirely yours if you don't work out. So forget about the male-female thing and just remember that we're making war, not love. I'm the boss—and that has nothing to do with male-female, either. You do what I say when I say it and we'll get along fine. We may even remain alive. Understood?"

"Okay," she replied soberly. "But do we have to scowl all the time?"

He said, "Wear your own face the way you like it and leave me to mine. Anyway, we won't be seeing that much of each other. You'll be staying with the plane until it's time to airlift this rig again."

"That's a mistake."

"What?"

"It's a mistake. Mr. Brognola warned me that you would—look, if it's not the sex then what is it? I'm a trained operative. I can be a real help to you."

"Trained how?" he inquired, seriously interested.

"Electronic intelligence. I can—"

"*Field* intelligence? Or are you an incubator baby?"

Color rushed to that lovely face. "I had field problems at the academy. But this is the first practical—"

He asked, "Can you climb a pole?"

She tucked that firm little chin into a pert nod of the head. "Like a monkey."

"Know how to tap into telephone carriers?"

"That's kindergarten stuff."

He sniffed. "It's going to be dangerous as hell."

"I know that."

The Bolan decision was characteristically quick, as much from the gut as from the head. "Okay. We'll try it. But get out of that jumpsuit and into something feminine. Don't downplay that fabulous body. A good soldier uses every tool available."

She was already stripping it off. "What exactly does that mean, Striker?"

He turned his head, more for his own peace of mind than as a concession to modesty. He growled at her, perhaps to cover the effect this

24

lady was having on him. "If you're a good soldier, you'll figure it out for yourself. Just don't ask me to be your conscience. The object is to get the job done and come out alive. That's the whole object."

The technically nude young lady was moving toward the rear of the motorhome. "In which order?"

He growled, "What?"

"You said get the job done and come out alive. If there's a conflict between those two, which comes first?"

She was slithering into a silky, formfitting chemise. And it was quite a form to be fitted. Bolan told her, "That's nice."

She said, "Please note that I brought it with me. Also—you haven't answered my question. Which comes first?"

He very soberly addressed her question. "There's no formula for that decision, April. It comes from the gut, not the head. If your gut is reliable then you'll never have to ponder the question. If it's not, then you're in the wrong line of work."

"Trying to scare me off?" she inquired quietly.

"Maybe," he admitted.

She stepped into delicate little shoes and said, "Okay, I'm fittingly frightened as well as fittingly dressed. And I'm still in. Aren't I?"

She was. But deeply enough only to allow the lady to feel useful and worthy. Bolan had no intention of testing April Rose's combat guts.

None whatever. He'd seen too many fail the test. And some of those, yeah, had been every bit as pretty and talented as April Rose . . . before the test.

CHAPTER 3

ON TRACK

The Ford was in tow behind the warwagon and the track had been due north from Louisville on interstate Route 65. The C-130 aircraft had been ordered on to Indianapolis, there to await further flight instructions.

Bolan wore faded blue denims, a sweatshirt, ankle-high moccasins. April Rose was seated at his right hand. She'd doodled theoretical problems in solid state mechanics on a scratch pad through much of the hour-long drive from Louisville. The conversation had been sparse and light, all of it initiated by the girl.

As they peeled away from the interstate at Columbus, she said to him, "You're not much of a talker, are you?"

He replied, "Not much, no." He flicked a glance at her scratch pad as he added, "I guess I've been doodling, too."

"In your head?"

"Yeah—if that's what you call it."

She sighed. "Sometimes it helps to talk. When we get time, let's—would you look at that! Did you see that signboard?"

"City marker?" he grunted.

"Yes, but did you see what they called it? The Athens of the Prairie. Is this a prairie?"

He replied with a grin. "Well, it is pretty flat."

"Have you ever been to Athens?"

He smiled and shook his head.

"Neither have I. But this looks nothing like the pictures I've seen."

He suggested, "Maybe it has something to do with the frame of mind."

"It certainly can't be the architecture," she said wrinkling her nose. "This is pure Midwestern Gothic."

Bolan chuckled and pushed the command console toward her. It was sort of nice, for a change, to have a companion. "Punch it up on the navigator," he suggested. "She knows all, tells all."

"What's the program?"

Bolan gave the lady the program as they crossed the White River and entered the downtown area. It was not a bad little town, after all, prairie or not. Many signs of recent construction—a new downtown mall rising in the shadow of an ancient cupola and spire courthouse—a modern new post office building with trick glass walls nestled alongside

28

crumbling warehouses of an earlier era—all, somehow, very appealing and inviting.

"There are signs of progress," he told the girl.

"I bet I can tell you why, too," she replied as she scanned the monitor display. "Lots of money here. Columbus is the home of the diesel engine. The man who developed it lived here. Cummins Engine seems to be the lifeblood of the area. Many other plants, too. It's not Athens, Striker. It's little Detroit."

"What's the crime pattern?" he asked absently.

"Saturday night stuff," she replied, sniffing. "Nothing I can see here to intrigue a man like Tuscanotte."

"Drugs?"

"A little action there. Grass, mostly, sez here. Usual small town pattern. The local cops are pretty tough on it. It says Indiana has a paraphernalia law. A two-ounce bust would probably make the local headlines. All in all, looks pretty clean."

"Gambling?" Bolan inquired, his mind only partially into it.

"The same. Small time. Football pool cards and the like. Indianapolis distributors, though. Nothing very exciting. Same for prostitution. Very disorganized, local girls, massage parlor quality. I really can't see a thing here for Tuscanotte."

"That's why he's here," Bolan told her.

"Low profile, huh?"

29

"You've got it. No profile whatever, actually. The guy dug a ditch and buried himself in it."

"In a prairie Athens," she added.

"It's still in the shadow of Chicago," Bolan pointed out. "It's a marvelous age, April. Ninety minutes or so by fast plane and he's right back in the homegrounds." He pulled the big rig into a public parking lot. "Or ten seconds by telephone. The phone will be easier to find. Go find it, Tinkerbell."

She smiled tolerantly. "What'd you call me?"

"Be a nice fairy and go find the telephone. Just be sure that no one knows what you're after."

She said, "You'd better drag that station wagon out of the street or the Prairie Athens police will show you what they're after."

He watched her halfway to the telephone company building, then sighed and pulled the Ford on into the parking lot, blocking off several meters in the process. A meter maid walked by, eyeing the tandem vehicles with casual interest. He stepped outside and fed coins into the meters, grinned at the lady, and went back inside. Then he smoked a cigarette and studied the area map display on the console while April Rose did her stuff in the Bell offices.

The city seemed adequately served by a network of highways in addition to the interstate route. Nice location, really. Louisville an hour south, Cincinnatti an hour east, Indianapolis and that great interstate hub less than an hour north. There was a small airport and an auxiliary naval air station nearby.

The general layout of the town itself, though, seemed rather chaotic, with state roads and a U.S. highway traversing the inner city in virtually every direction. The business district was very compact, encompassing just a few square blocks, with outlying shopping centers grouped northeasterly, and industrial development to the south—except for Cummins—which appeared to dominate the city proper. The river rather effectively curtailed western expansion except for a tourist-related buildup at the accesses to the interstate highway.

West of the interstate route was entirely rural, with some rather dramatic terrain variations. No prairie that way. About fifteen miles to the west lay the village of Nashville and a large state park, in an area called "the little Smokies." Interesting names on the map that way: Gnaw Bone, Stone Head, Bean Blossom, Stoney Lonesome. It sounded like frontier country.

Bolan was playing a little mind game with himself when April Rose returned from her mission. He had adjusted the area display to the region west of Columbus, focusing on the route to Gnaw Bone.

The girl moved in beside him and said, "Okay, Striker, I found the phone."

He immediately fired the engine and eased out of the parking lot, heading back along the reverse course. "I heard your words," he told her, "but your face is saying something different."

"Well I nearly blew it. Have you heard of ACF?"

He shook his head. "What is that—a company?"

"No, it's a new Bell System service. It means Automatic Call Forwarding. Anyone can have it for a few bucks a month. If you subscribe to that service, you can program automatic call forwarding from your own telephone. I mean, you program it yourself. You don't tell anyone but your own telephone. It does the rest, via computerized switching circuits at the phone company. Any incoming calls will be automatically diverted to any telephone in the country that you may choose. The calling party would never have to know that the call had been diverted. If it's a local diversion, the monthly service fee takes care of it. If long distance, the call is metered to your base phone and charged like any toll call."

"What are you telling me, April?"

"I'm telling you that the Columbus number is a dummy, a robot number. I don't believe we'll find your friend Tuscanotte in Columbus."

"Me either," Bolan said quietly.

"The dummy is in a crummy little two by four office above a downtown store front. The subscriber is listed—what'd you say?"

"I said, me either."

She had just become aware of their position in the traffic flow. They were crossing the river

32

again, headed back toward the interstate route. "What are you doing?" she asked, very quietly.

"Listening to your report," he assured her. "Keep on."

"But you're already—I haven't told you— you already knew!"

He shook his head. "Educated guess only. I do need your report, Tinkerbell."

"Dammit I wish you wouldn't call me that!" she flared.

He said, very softly, "Okay. No disrespect intended—believe it. I'm very impressed with what you're saying. Can I hear the rest of it?"

She snatched a cigarette from the console and lit it. Not until they'd reached the Holiday Inn, at the I-65 ramp, did she speak. "Go straight ahead," she instructed. "Stay on state route 46."

Instead, he pulled into the motel and drove to the back lot where he unhitched the Ford and parked it.

The girl was giving him a speculative gaze as he returned to the con and again headed out on 46 west.

"Had me scared for a minute, there, boss," she said quietly.

He very soberly told her, "Perish the thought. There's nothing indirect about me, April. You'll always know precisely what I want from you."

"Fair enough," she replied, matching his sobriety.

They passed under the interstate route and picked up speed.

33

The girl said, "I'm sorry. Where was I?"

He told her, "You were in a crummy little office with a dummy telephone."

"Right. It's listed as R.B. Smith Company. That's all, no amplifying remarks. The bills are paid by postal money order, under the same name. I got the rest by blind luck. The girl in the telephone office knows the man who owns the building where R.B. Smith is located. Thank God for small towns. She said that the R.B. Smith Company is quite a mystery. The office was rented several months ago, the lease paid for six months in advance, the telephone installed—and since then no one has seen hide nor hair of R.B. Smith. Then I happened to notice the little billing code and saw that R.B. Smith was paying for ACF services. And here's the part that hurts. I'd never *heard* of ACF. Had you?"

Bolan said, "It's a quick world, April."

"You bet it is. Well, then—look—I had to lean on my badge."

"Small towns work in both directions," he quietly told her.

"I know that. But I had to get into that computer and find the program. They were very helpful. Don't worry. I covered it with a good story. And I got what we need. Or I guess you need it. Do you?"

"I'm working straight from the gut. Sure I need it."

"Okay." She made a teasing face. "But first I want to know how your gut sent you in this direction."

34

He shrugged. "I really couldn't tell you that. I was looking at the sector display. My gut lurched west. Then you came back with your eyes rolling westward."

"Aw. They were not."

He chuckled. "They sure weren't saying Columbus."

She said, "You're scary—know that? Okay, slow down. I believe we turn left at this next—yes, that's the road. Go south."

Bolan turned the warwagon south. Soon thereafter they were rolling past a rather immodest stone structure set high on a hill overlooking the surrounding countryside. A gravelled drive peeled away from the blacktop road at a very small angle, then climbed the hill in a series of switchbacks.

Said the lady, "I'll bet that's the place. How does the old gut feel about it?"

He asked, "Is this as far as the head can move us?"

She replied, "I'm afraid so. We're certainly in the general area. But I'd have to get out and read some line codes to—"

"Never mind." Bolan halted the vehicle and backed along the road. "We'll just drive up and ask them."

"Are you serious?"

He was. He angled onto the gravel drive and climbed the hill to the house. Almost to the house. The hilltop was larger and flatter than it had appeared from the roadway. Several smaller buildings could now be seen clustered about the main structure. The whole thing was densely wooded but there were no walls or fences in evidence. Only a chain, supported by waist-high metal gateposts, blocked vehicular entrance to the compound. "No Trespassing" signs were posted and a small turnaround had been provided.

Bolan pulled into the turnaround as he asked the lady, "What name is R.B. Smith using here?"

"Roger G. Tucker. That's pretty close to—uh oh!"

A guy wearing a bright orange hunting vest and toting a double-barreled shotgun had suddenly appeared at the chain barrier. Bolan donned dark glasses, growled, "Stay put," to the girl, and made a quick exit.

He called an amiable greeting to the guy at the chain and strolled over for a parley.

"Who'd you want?" the sentry inquired, not at all amiable.

"I'm looking for Gene Harney," Bolan lied.

"Wrong place," the guy growled.

"Do you know Gene? He lives somewhere in this—"

"Never heard of him. You're trespassing. Get lost."

Bolan said, "Hey—I asked a civil question."

"You got a civil answer, bub." The shotgun came up. "Beat it."

Bolan quietly retreated to the motorhome. He told the girl, "Bingo," and put that place behind them.

"Tucker is Tuscanotte?" she asked nervously.

"I couldn't swear to it," Bolan replied. "But I was just jawing with Skids Mangone. And he's a long way from home."

"Who is Mangone?"

"Used to break legs in Chicago for Joliet Jake Vecci."

"Well who is Vecci?"

"Vecci is no more," Bolan explained. "But he was the Lord of the Loop for many years—in Chicago, you know. And he was an uncle by marriage to Carmine Tuscanotte."

"I'd call that pretty conclusive," she said.

"So would I," Bolan agreed.

The lady's eyes were fairly dancing. "So what do we do now?"

Bolan had no need to ask himself that question.

Indeed, there was no question.

He knew precisely what had to be done.

CHAPTER 4

WISE GUY

Harry Venturi had come by his "Apeman" tag honestly. He had the torso, arms and shoulders of a six-footer but from the hips down the guy was strictly five-foot material. In the trade-off between the two halves, the whole man emerged as a rather curiously constructed five-and-a-half footer who appeared to be all torso and arms. There was no deformation but only a quite noticeable mismatch between the two halves.

He had not been kidded about that since early in his youth. And nobody breathed Apeman within his earshot—though, of course, he knew how the Mob had tagged him. It was okay with Venturi, so long as nobody said it to his face.

He and Skids Mangone had come the long way together, moving progressively through a succession of connections from the juvenile street gangs to within the very shadow of the underworld throne of power. They'd made the whole trip on simple savagery. Neither had ever worked a legitimate job. Mangone was technically illiterate but had found his rightful place in an environment where brutality bred respect. Venturi had a bit more cunning and could read with understanding the editorial page of the *Chicago Tribune;* also, he seemed to have a natural ability to pick winners and to alter connections at advantageous moments. And, yes, the two had come the long way together. But . . . to where? To this joint in the sticks? Was *this* success?

Things would never again be the same in Chicago. He knew that. This was a sort of exile—a self-imposed exile, on the part of his current boss. And Venturi felt that it was no answer to the problems at home. Problems had a way of following a guy. They'd followed Carmine all the way to Kentucky, hadn't they? And maybe that was just a beginning.

He was staring at the telephone and wondering why no further word had come from Ben David when Mangone—officially the yard boss at this encampment—came through the kitchen door and went straight to the coffee pot.

"What was it?" Venturi grunted.

"The same," replied his old sidekick.

"Another camper, eh?"

"Yeah. Had a smart mouth, too. Wise bastard. We ought to start shooting these smart-asses. Belt 'em around some, anyway. Then they'd think twice about tramping around on other people's turf."

"What'd he look like?"

"Huh?"

"The camper."

Mangone carried his coffee to the table and sat down as he replied, "Like all the rest. 'Cept his RV was a bit snazzier. I shoulda shot the son of a bitch and kept that RV. Think I'll get me one of those, Harry. You ever been inside one of those? Hell, they got everything in there. They got—"

"How many boys you got out?"

"Huh?"

"Who's on watch?"

"Buck Jones and Hopalong Cassidy."

Venturi was feeling very edgy. "*Them* two. I thought you told me you was going to split those boys up."

"Aw, they're okay, Harry. Like you'n me in the old days. Full of piss and vinegar."

Venturi did not reply to that.

"You know they got toilets and everything in those—even a shower? They even got—"

"I think we better double up."

"Huh?"

"You better put all the boys out. Make sure their radios work. We get any more *campers*, I want to see them before they're let go."

Mangone was unhappy with that decision. "Hell, Harry, just because we got hit in Kentucky don't mean—that's a long ways off. It don't mean—"

"Don't tell me what it don't mean," Venturi

said harshly. "We take no chances till we find out what it *does* mean. Get it hard. Right now."

He disliked using that tone of voice on his old buddy from the southside. But it had the desired effect. It started the adrenalin flowing through the big dummy.

Mangone's eyes narrowed to mere slits as he muttered, "Right—I gotcha, Harry." He finished his coffee with a quick gulp, snatched up his shotgun, and went back outside.

Venturi carried his coffee to the kitchen window and watched as his yard boss moved purposefully toward the cabins at the rear. Some yard boss. Skids Mangone and his fearless crew of four piss-and-vinegar cowboys. They'd asked for horses for their patrols. Shit! Not a one of 'em had ever sat on a horse in his whole life. Who'd feed the damn things, and water them, and clean up their damn mess? *Those* cowboys?

He shook his head over the thought of it. Yeah. Things had been going to hell for a long time. It wasn't like the old days. Fuckin' goddam Bolan. Things had never been right since ... well ... it wasn't *all* Bolan. The Outfit itself was going soft. Those kids back there would grumble and bellyache like hell about being rousted this soon after their nightwatch. So let 'em bellyache. It was about time they learned what life is like when you hire your guns to the highest bidder. They'd had it too damned easy for too damned long. A little ex-

41

tra watch wouldn't hurt 'em none. And Harry Venturi would kick some asses if they—

Something was wrong!

A few harsh words had not moved Mangone's adrenalin *that* much. The big dummy came stumbling around the end cabin with his shotgun at the shoulder and whirling.

Venturi instinctively ducked as the double-barrels swung across his line of vision. Hell, that guy could send a load of shot any damned place he wanted it to go. But there was no report. Skids wasn't *shooting*—he was . . .

Venturi made a break for the outside door and edged cautiously through it, his pistol at the ready. "What is it?" he called to the disturbed yard boss.

Mangone had taken shelter in a clump of trees new the corner of the house. "I don't know," he called back. "Stay indoors, Harry."

"What is it, dammit!"

"It's Arnold and Piccolo. Dead in their beds. Throats cut."

Venturi snarled, "Get in here, Skids! Come on! I'll cover you!"

The yard boss tucked it in and made a run for it. But there was no challenge to that run. Venturi shoved his friend inside and quickly followed, going immediately to a two-way radio, which sat on the kitchen drainboard. "Hoppy—Buck!" he yelled into the microphone. "Check in, dammit!"

Mangone had gone on through and was standing at the living room windows. "Nothing moving out here, Harry," he reported.

42

"Hoppy! Buck!"

He tried again and turned the receiver squelch control all the way to zero, but there was no response to the radio summons.

"Well shit!" Venturi yelled. He spun to the doorway and called to his old partner who'd come all the way with him, "I get nothing from outside! What've you got?"

"I got nothing, Harry," was the worried response. "What do you think it is?"

"The cowboys," Venturi replied with a sigh. "I never felt right about those boys. They cut Arnold and Piccolo and split."

"Why?"

"Why not? Somebody has set us up, Skids. Hell, *you* should recognize it."

"You think it's tied to Kentucky?"

"I know it is. They're after Carmine. And they screwed it up. They think he's here. They'll be coming in. It's time we did some thinking, you'n me."

"What're we thinking about, Harry?"

"Connections. This one suddenly stinks. We need to think about it."

"Whatever you say is okay with me," was the taut reply from the front windows.

Venturi went in there and stood by the stairway in agonizing indecision for a long moment, then said, "I say let's give it to 'em. What the hell are we protecting? It's not as if—maybe we can play it both ways."

The big dummy turned from the windows to say, "Carmine will be coming back, Harry. He'll walk right into it."

43

"Not if we can get out and warn him."

"Okay," said Mangone, reaching his decision without apparent difficulty. "I'll go out and get a car ready. Cover me, then come on out when I honk."

"Better not," Venturi growled. "They could be—we'll have a better chance if we hoof it out the back way."

"God it could be a long walk."

"Could be a damn short one, too. You got plenty of shells for that blunderbuss?"

The dummy cradled the shotgun in the crooks of both arms to pat his vest. "I got plenty, yeah," he reported. Then he did something very peculiar. His eyes flared and locked themselves onto dead space several feet above Venturi's head, as though that clouded mind had suddenly gone off somewhere to play. Then he knelt on the floor, going down very slowly, and carefully deposited the shotgun, allowing it to slide off his forearms without a sound.

A voice behind and above, from the stairway, called down, "You too, Venturi. Drop the piece and show me your smiling face—quickly, very quickly."

Harry the Apeman felt very little like smiling. But he did drop the revolver, very quickly, and turned a pained countenance to that bloodchilling voice.

He was a big guy—a very big guy—all togged out like a guy in some war movie in a black combat suit; belts and shit strung all over him, knives and guns and chokestrings, even a couple of grenades. More chilling than

44

anything, though, was a giant silver blaster hanging there in the guy's big paw like they were made for each other and the damndest, hardest eyes backing it all up Harry Venturi had ever seen.

There was no need to wonder about anything, now.

The whole story was standing there on that stairway, blowing death at him through the eyes. He'd never seen this guy before, of course, but there was no doubting the obvious.

"Hi, Bolan," he said weakly.

"Hi, Harry," said the Executioner. "Where's Carmine?"

"He ain't here," said the big dummy with the fearsome shotgun at his knees.

"I can see that, Skids," the guy said. The voice was not all that mean. It was just . . . *deadly*. A small metal object fell to the floor at the bottom of the stairs. Yeah. The guy's marker . . . a death medal, the dreaded bull's-eye-across, symbol of the marksman. "I brought him a gift. I can as easily leave it with you boys."

At least the guy was talking, not shooting. According to the stories, that was a hopeful sign.

But Skids, the big dummy, had it read all wrong. Mangone had come the long way—at Venturi's coattails—and he's made a place for himself where brutality earned respect.

There was no visible respect, here, now.

And Skids just couldn't read it. The big dummy made a sudden dive for his shotgun,

45

stupid to the very end, deaf to the despairing plea for sanity from his lifelong chum who'd managed to keep him alive and functioning all these years, dead before clawing fingers even reached his equalizer.

The silver pistol had thundered but once, battering the ears and stunning the senses.

The dummy's head virtually exploded in midair, parts of it spraying off toward the windows while the remainder swung the whole body like a bulldogged calf flopping to earth on its back.

Harry the Apeman remained precisely where he'd been when the moment of truth overtook him, quickly averting his eyes from that horror on the floor, but otherwise frozen, barely breathing.

But there was no second thunderclap.

Instead, that same insistent voice with a question which would not be denied: "Where's Carmine, Harry?"

So . . . what the hell. Things had been going sour for a long time. Satisfying connections had been hard to come by and even harder to hang onto. All the pleasures of being a wise guy were fading away, replaced by grim survival in a world beginning to eat itself.

And what was a wise guy, after all?

He was a guy who knew how to survive.

Harry the Apeman Venturi had made an art of survival. And now he had to be smart for only one. He spread his hands and showed a sick smile to the big stoney guy on the stairs.

46

"It's been a long road, Mr. Bolan," he said tiredly. "I'm ready to get off."

Yeah. Damn right. Harry Venturi was not going to die stupid.

CHAPTER 5

FEELINGS

She was not real sure about her feelings for the big grim man. Oh sure—*physically,* there were no doubts. God, he was the sexiest thing she'd ever encountered. She tingled just to look at him. But she was not so sure about the other side of the coin. What sort of man did it take to do the things he'd done? How could a man be so . . . so *gentle* one moment and . . . and then go out to do the—what he did—without a grimace of regret, without . . . well, without what, April?

What do you want from the man, anyway—an apology?—a prayer for forgiveness?—a melancholy look? Would that make it holy and right?

She'd come into it with eyes wide open, of course—sure, she'd *leapt* at the chance! And she'd known all that was public knowledge about this remarkable man. More than that, Hal Brognola himself had briefed her for two solid hours. She'd known, sure. But somehow it was different to read about it, to hear about it—and then to come face to face with the reality of it.

Mack Bolan was a killer.

He was not a cop or a spy or anything official. He went around, on his own, killing people. A self-appointed executioner.

And boy did he look the part!

That had probably been the moment of truth for April Rose—when she saw Mack Bolan transform himself from Mr. Quiet and Gentle to Mr. Executioner. The black outfit—how symbolic!—the combat rig with all those grim weapons of death, the sudden coldness in those deep, deep eyes and the pantherlike grace of his movements as he prepared for his mission.

"What are you doing?" she'd inquired innocently, thirty seconds after they pulled away from Tuscanotte's hideaway.

But it was very obvious what he was doing. He'd parked the big vehicle at the bottom of the hill and gone back to his armory to select weapons for the kill.

The moment of truth, sure. Off with the casual clothing and—how handy!—there's the black union suit already in place and awaiting the accessories.

Some accessories.

"What are those things?" she'd asked timidly, pointing to the little shoestringlike coils dangling from the chest harness.

"Garrotes," he'd replied, in a voice already growing cold.

"Garrotes," she echoed faintly. "You, uh, choke people with them."

"It's a quite kill," he'd explained with no emotion whatever.

"As opposed to the hand grenades," she said.

"The grenades are insurance."

"Against what?"

"Against being pinned down and unable to withdraw. I don't really know what's up there, you see."

Yes, she saw. But also she did not see. "Then why go up there?"

"To see what's there," he replied.

Like the climber who scales mountains because they are there.

Sure.

April Rose was feeling just a bit faint, at that point. The whole moment had suddenly become entirely unreal. What was it about the human male that sent him constantly in quest of his own manhood? What primeval instinct lurked within manly breasts to send sturdy, vital young men hurling themselves constantly into one senseless challenge after another? If the world had been a rose garden . . . well, maybe it had been, at one time. And it hadn't been the woman who caused the fall from grace. It had been a vital, reckless male animal who saw thorns instead of roses.

April told her male animal, "We know what's there. Why don't we just report it out.

We've found him. Let Washington take it from here."

"Where would Washington take it?" he asked quietly, without a pause from his preparations for war.

"They'll take it—they'll come out here with warrants, they will—"

He was almost smiling as he broke into that confused reply. "Tuscanotte isn't hiding from the law, April. He's hiding from his own kind. He's under no indictments and officially the law has no interest in him. But even if you could get a warrant, and even if you could make an arrest, he'd be back on the streets within twenty minutes. And even if somehow you actually managed to get him behind bars, he'd go right on running his little empire by remote control. Our system was never designed for people like these. That's why the Tuscanottes are so successful. And that's why I work outside the system."

It was quite along speech, considering the source. And he was ready for his EVA when he finished it. He enclosed her whole face in the gentle clasp of one huge hand and kissed her quickly on the lips, then told her, "Take the cruiser on around the curve and park it off the road. Activate the optic systems and get a picture of everything entering and leaving. If you're approached, take off. If I'm not back in thirty minutes, take off. In either event, I'll meet you at the Holiday Inn in Columbus . . . when I can."

She asked, breathlessly, "And if you don't—you don't?"

He smiled soberly as he told her, "Then you call Brognola and tell him that John Phoenix sends regrets to the President. He'll understand."

"Who is John Phoenix?"

"Someone not yet born," was the cryptic reply.

And then the remarkable man had stepped outside and instantly disappeared into the dense timber.

Leaving April Rose to fuss and fume at herself over a mixed bag of seething emotions.

She really did not approve of what this man was doing. And she would never understand the government's motives in condoning such activities, however unofficial that support may be. But as she sat at the optics monitor and stewed in her own emotions, she began to get a clue about all that.

They condoned the actions, maybe, because they loved the man.

That was possible, sure.

And maybe she did, too. Love the man, that is. Physically, for damn sure. And perhaps a bit deeper than that. Already, yes, maybe quite a bit deeper than that.

Dammit.

She would *not* give her heart to a man who had not one of his own.

"So where is he, Harry?"

"Look, I wouldn't juke you around. I'm not

that stupid. You got to believe that. I don't know exactly where he is right at the moment. I can't even contact him. He pulled out of here two days ago—just him and his tagmen. Willie Frio and Fuzz Martin. You know of those guys? They been with Carmine since Day One. He had some meetings set up—some important business parleys—up north somewheres. I think one up in Lafayette, another in Anderson. Those are towns here in Indiana."

"So when is he coming back?"

"Today. He's coming back today. But not here. I mean, not straight back here. He's going over to Nashville first. That's only about ten or fifteen minutes from here. Not Tennessee. Indiana Nashville, *little* Nashville. They even got a little opry house over there."

"Is he singing at the opry today, Harry?"

"Ha ha. No, not him. You should hear him in the bathtub. Thinks he's Mario Lanza but that voice wouldn't sell fish."

"So what's in little Nashville for Carmine?"

"Another parley. Very important. Some bigshots from Indianapolis. You know, state guys."

"Uh huh. Where does he usually hold these parleys?"

"You mean in Nashville?"

"Isn't that where we're talking about?"

"Guess I lost my mind for a minute there. I wasn't stalling, Bolan. He usually goes to the Ramada Inn. He likes the prime rib there."

"A little village like that has a Ramada Inn?"

53

"Oh sure. Hey, it's a tourist spot. People come from all around, even tour buses and all that. They get about a jillion people in there every year. October is best. October is crazy, I hear."

"What's the attraction?"

"Trees. Autumn trees."

"Autumn trees? Come on, Harry. What are you—"

"No, seriously. I mean, that's why October, but they got other—they got a Dillinger museum there."

"That's very interesting."

"Yeah, I thought so too. John Dillinger. He was an Indiana boy, you know. You ought to catch that. Very interesting. FBI guy."

"What FBI guy?"

"An FBI guy owns the museum. Or maybe he's not FBI now, I dunno. But it's worth seeing."

"Tour buses and everything, eh?"

"Well that's just one—that's—they got art galleries and all that."

Bolan chuckled. "You're quite an entertainer, Harry."

"No, I swear." Venturi chuckled, also. "I guess it's an art colony or something. These hills are swarming with easels and paintbrushes. Also they do all kinds of native crafts. I don't mean Africa native, I mean Indiana native, pioneer stuff, you know? They even still live in log cabins around there. They got a jail that must be five hundred years old, I swear. God, I would've hated to do time in that joint."

"Let's see if I have you straight now, Harry. We have autumn trees and tour buses and a John Dillinger museum owned by an FBI guy. And we got art galleries and pioneers and a thousand-year-old jail. So people come from all around, about a jillion a year, to keep the Ramada Inn full. That right?"

"You got it. And they got another big resort hotel there, too. But Carmine likes the prime rib at the Ramada."

"That's why he holds his business parleys there."

"Yeah."

"Who's he meeting there today?"

"Like I said, these bigshots from the state capital. He's trying to juice a couple of things."

"Like what?"

"Well—like Indiana just passed a racetrack bill."

"They've been racing in Indianapolis as long as I can remember, Harry."

"No I mean horse racing."

"Carmine thinking of building a track?"

"Naw, that's too much to juice and not enough return. It's too regulated. Carmine wants the concessions."

"They're building this track in Nashville?"

"Oh, I don't know about that. It's a local option bill. See, each county has got to pass its own bill. Then if that passes it goes to the state racing commission. That's where the decision

55

is made. It's a regulating thing, see, to keep down the number of tracks—to keep them from choking each other out, see. But Carmine says Nashville would be a natural for racing."

"Well it's already got an opry and autumn trees and all that—right?"

"I guess that's why, yeah. Actually I guess he don't give a shit where. He just wants the concessions—wherever. That's where the money's at, see."

"So he's meeting these people at the Ramada?"

"Yeah."

"When?"

"I said today."

"I said today when."

"God, I'm not sure exactly when."

"Let's review the ground rules, Harry."

"What ground rules?"

"The ones keeping you alive and me happy. I don't like you, Harry. I don't like anything you stand for. You're a parasite who never once in his life built anything, or preserved anything, or accomplished anything worthwhile for the world at large. Do you agree with that?"

"I guess that's about right, Mr. Bolan. I guess so."

"Uh huh. That's the ground rule. The weight of guys like you, hanging on and sucking from everything that's right and decent in the world is just too damn much for the world to bear. To see you standing here sucking air right now is almost too much for *me* to bear. But it's nothing personal. I don't even know your mother's name—whether she breastfed you or tossed you bologna on the floor—so you see I don't really know a thing about you . . . as a person. But I know *what* you are, Harry, and that disturbs me very much. I step around cockroaches to keep from squashing them. But I don't step around people like you. Okay?"

"Okay, sure, I understand perfectly. You hate my guts. I can understand that."

"I don't hate your guts, Harry. I just can't live on the same planet with them. I draped garrotes on your two outside boys and I opened the throats on the sleeping beauties out back. You saw what I did to your old pal Skids. Why do you think I haven't done the same to you?"

"Because you—because I . . ."

"Ground rules. If I blast, you can't talk. If you talk, I can't blast. That's a ground rule, Harry. It overrides my natural desire to rid the planet of your weight. It's called a truce, a white flag parley. Do you kapish?"

"I kapish, sure."

"Have you ever heard of me violating a white flag?"

"No sir. I always heard just the opposite."

"That's because I've never violated one. But I've never been conned into one, either. Know why? Because I've been into too many guts just like yours. And I know crap when I smell it, guy. Right now I'm smelling crap. Do we have a flag or don't we?"

"Okay, you're right—you're right. I don't know why, either—that son of a bitch never gave me nothing but scraps off his table. I don't know why it's so hard to—you can understand that though, I know. Okay. No more crap. Carmine is meeting these guys at the Ramada at three o'clock, give or take a few minutes. That's his exact words: give or take a few minutes. They're meeting at the bar. You have to watch it because he always sends his tagmen in first to case the joint. And you'll never see those guys unless you're watching real close. They don't stand *around* him. They are very savvy boys so watch your ass. He'll have dinner after the parley. Then back here probably by seven or eight o'clock."

"How many in his party?"

"Like I said, three. Him and the two tagmen."

"You're sure of that."

"That's the way he always goes. And he's always back by seven or eight."

"What's Carmine's name?"

"Huh? Oh I see what—Tucker. He's using Roger Tucker."

"How's his love life?"

"He never brings any of it here. But he's always talking about this blonde or that blonde. I guess he gets it all on the road."

"Does he ever get it at the Ramada in Nashville?"

"In Bloomington sometimes, I think."

"What is Bloomington?"

"That's a college town about twenty miles on past Nashville, west of Nashville. They call it Beaver City on the CB. I don't know, maybe ten or twenty thousand cute little things going

58

to school there. Indiana University—the Hurrying Hoosiers, you know. Basketball."

"You talking to rattle my brain, Harry?"

"No. I guess I'm just nervous. You wanted to know his love life. He gets some in Bloomington, I think. I don't know if it's college stuff or not. I heard it's pretty loose on prostitution over there, though. Helluva thing, I say. It's a college town, I mean."

Bolan said, "You worry about such things, huh?"

"You think I can't? You think I'm really like you say? All the way through? Listen, I could have a kid going to school there right now. I got kids, yeah. Haven't seen 'em since they were in diapers but I got 'em. Yeah, I worry about those things."

"What am I going to do with you, Harry?"

"Huh?"

"How can we seal this deal? If I let you off—how do I know what you're going to do between now and three o'clock?"

"I won't be heading towards Nashville, that's for damn sure."

"Telephones are cheap."

"I wouldn't spend a dime for that guy, Mr. Bolan."

"Or to get even with me?"

"We're even already. I wouldn't do that."

"Why not?"

"Like I said, we're even. Also 'cause I don't think Carmine is man enough to whack you. And I don't want you coming looking for me.

59

No sir. Not ever again. If I'm off the hook, then I'm staying off. I'm not stupid."

"Is he pushing dope on campus, Harry?"

"Who?"

"Carmine."

"What'd you ask me?"

"Is Carmine bankrolling the push in Bloomington?"

"Not much, I think."

"How much is not much?"

"A little coke, maybe some chemicals. Nothing big. They already got a circuit over there. I think he maybe financed a couple of small buys in the Caribbean that found its way to Bloomington. But he's very leery of the stuff. Nothing to do with conscience, just prison bars. He's too cagey to risk the big fall."

"You're not stupid, eh?"

"I try not to be."

"Does Carmine have a woman in Nashville?"

"Nothing regular, no."

"But she meets him sometimes at the Ramada. After the prime rib."

"Sometimes, I think. Probably."

"Don't say it because you think I want to hear it. Say it because you know it."

"Okay. I know it."

"You didn't know it a couple minutes ago."

"It slipped my mind. Look, this is all very nervous for me. You know how long I been staring up the muzzle of that big blaster?"

"What's the lady's name?"

"All I get is Jackie."

"Jackie?"

60

"Yeah, like Jackie Onassis. Only of course not. I think he imported her from around Chicago. She wants to be an artist, I get. Takes lessons there in Nashville. Carmine got her a cabin in the hills somewheres outside of town. Oh. It has an overlook. She calls it the studio. Ten lessons and she's got herself a studio already."

"You've met her?"

"Not—no. He brought her by here once. She stayed in the car while he came in for something. I didn't see much of her."

"Young and pretty?"

"Sure. Carmine wouldn't get caught dead with anything but. A snazzy blonde, that's all I caught."

"Three o'clock at the Ramada?"

"That's right."

"The flag comes down in two minutes, Harry. Make sure you're not around when it does."

"You saying goodbye and farewell?"

"You got it. But Harry . . . remember the ground rules. And remember that I didn't come to Indiana to get whacked by Carmine Tuscanotte. I don't intend to be. If I walk into something unhappy at Nashville, I'll know why. And I'll be looking for you, Harry."

"I never claimed to be the brightest guy in the world, Mr. Bolan. But I'm telling you I'm not stupid."

"Goodbye, Harry."

"I'll take one of the cars."

61

"Take whatever you want. Just do it within one minute and thirty seconds."

The guy still did not quite believe it. He walked out of there backwards, not for a moment removing the gaze from Bolan's cold eyes, then pivoted into a full gallop from the doorway.

Bolan heard an engine cough to life and a moment later tires chewing gravel along the drive.

So much for that.

And what had been gained?

Perhaps nothing.

But Bolan had the feeling that he would encounter Carmine Tuscanotte at three o'clock in Nashville. What else, and who else, may be encountered there was material for secondary speculation.

But the feeling in the gut was good.

The Executioner would be in little Nashville at three o'clock.

CHAPTER 6

FOUNDATIONS

Glistening eyes met him at the door as he stepped inside the cruiser. She said, "I was getting worried. A car came down about ten minutes ago. Went by me like a bat. I thought—well, I heard a shot a few minutes before that. Just one shot. I was afraid that . . ."

Bolan went on to the rear to shed the combat rig, telling her, "It went very well. No complications. The guy in the car was Harry Venturi. Tuscanotte wasn't there."

She said, rather breathlessly, "Oh," and just stood there rather awkwardly in the war room as he checked in the personal arsenal.

Bolan said, mainly to fill the silence, "Venturi cooperated. Or I hope he did. He says Tuscanotte will be in Nashville at three o'clock. A business meeting at the Ramada Inn." He flashed her a quick smile. "*Little* Nashville, that is—just west of here."

"Can we believe that?" she asked, rather mechanically.

"The gut says so," he told her.

"I have pictures of the car," she reported. "Actually I videotaped it. We have front, side, and rear coverage. About fifteen seconds worth. If you need it."

He replied, "Yes, that's good. I'll want to take a look at that." He stripped off his blouse and gave her an oblique gaze. "I'm going to take a navy shower."

She pulled the blank gaze away from him and turned rather stiffly toward the bow of the cruiser. He finished undressing and moved into the tiny shower stall. "May as well get us moving," he called out to her. "We'll go to Columbus first and pick up your vehicle."

The girl gave no verbal response to that but a moment later they were underway.

Bolan quickly washed away the stains of combat and was getting into fresh clothing before they reached the juncture with highway 46. He dropped down beside the girl and pulled the command console toward him.

There seemed to be no words between them. A tension, though, yeah, hung almost tangibly in the atmosphere separating those two seats.

He programmed the video for slow motion replay and ran the tape several times. The broadside coverage provided a rather good study of the fleeing vehicle plus its occupant in clear profile. It was the face of a defeated man,

64

not an elated one. It was enough to make the gut feel a bit better. He tried to share it with the girl.

He said, "Good job, April. I'll know that car if I see it again. And that's quite a study of Harry Venturi."

She ignored that completely, instead quietly inquiring, "What happened up there?"

Something was eating her, that was obvious. He replied, "Standard routine. I penetrated. Saw that Tuscanotte was not present. Conducted a search for physical intelligence and interrogated a prisoner. Ascertained the probable whereabouts of the mission target."

"Who got shot?"

"Is this a debriefing?" he asked lightly.

"Does it bother you to talk about it?"

No, it didn't bother him. Not in the way she was thinking. "Skids Mangone intercepted 240 grains of .44 Magnum immediately behind the left ear. That was at a distance of about twenty feet, so he absorbed more than a thousand foot-pounds of energy within a sphere incapable of containing it. In short, he died before he knew it."

She shivered and said, "Gross!"

Bolan said nothing. They were by now running east along highway 46 toward Columbus. A moment later, the girl said, "I noticed that two of your garrotes were missing. What are they? Disposables?"

He gave her a one-word reply. "Yes."

That pretty face wore no expression whatsoever. "What do you—how do they work?"

"You really want to know?"

"Yes."

"Why?"

"I'm just trying to understand you. Your business, I mean."

He replied, a bit drily, "And garrotes are my business, eh?"

"Well if you'd rather not talk about it . . ."

Bolan sighed and stared at the pretty lady for a long moment, then he told her, "Look, I know what your head is into. Mine has been there enough that I can recognize the atmosphere. But I want—"

"You don't have to justify anything to me," she said miserably.

"Wouldn't try to," he replied. "But there's something you need—"

"I don't want to talk about it," she protested.

Bolan said, "Okay. We won't talk about it. It was a bad idea to start with. We'll pick up your car then I want you to go on ahead to Indianapolis. Stick close to the plane. I want to be airborne again by midnight."

"That isn't fair!" the girl said angrily. "Our agreement was—"

"Fair has nothing to do with it," Bolan coldly told her. "This is no game of cops and robbers, good and bad. It's warfare, lady, and all the rules of war apply. Our agreement was that we'd give it a try. What we were trying was your belly for warfare. You don't have one. So you don't belong here. That's all the fair there is to it."

"That's a lot of bull!" she cried. "You al-

66

ready said that I did well. A good job, you called it. You're firing me because . . . because . . ."

"Because you're not a good cheerleader? Forget that, you're thinking like a kid. And maybe that's the whole problem. Well, no, that isn't fair—scratch it. The problem is that you don't have your head screwed on for this sort of assignment. That's neither good nor bad, it's just the way it is."

"What you mean is that I'm not the blood-thirsty type!" she replied nastily.

He showed her half a smile and said, "We're going to talk about it, eh?"

"Damn right we're going to talk about it!"

He said, "Go ahead."

"Just because I believe that life is sacred doesn't mean that I can't . . . that I . . ."

"That's a rather broad statement."

"What?"

"Life is sacred. Is that what you really mean?"

"Yes. Shall we begin our discussion there?"

"Begin with the elephant."

"Huh?"

"Life is sacred, you say. How 'bout the elephant?"

She said, "There are degrees of—but, yes, her life is sacred."

"And the flea on the elephant's back? Alive—so sacred?"

The lady was beginning to enjoy the conversation. A small smile accompanied the

67

response. "I bet I know where you're headed. I'll agree that the flea is life."

"But not sacred?"

"To another flea, maybe."

"You're playing the question," Bolan said. "You say the elephant is sacred because it's alive but there's some doubt about the flea. What's the problem? Is the elephant more alive than the flea?"

"She's a lot larger," said April Rose, twinkling just a bit.

"But we don't measure life by its size. Life is a *force*—isn't it? It pops out wherever it can. As an elephant—as a flea—as a flower."

"As a man or a woman," she added.

"So life is a force, really, not a thing."

"We're talking about different aspects, I believe," she replied. "I'm talking about men and women. Human life."

"So we're not really talking about the sanctity of *life*, then."

"Same thing," she said.

"You just said they were different."

"Mack, you cannot equate a flea with a man."

He grinned and said, "But the same thing that energizes the flea also energizes the man. At what point does that energy become sacred?"

"Oh, so now *life* is *energy*! Really!"

"Doesn't matter what you call it," he said. "If you agree that it's a constructive force. Do you?"

"Constructive? Not always."

"It starts that way, doesn't it. That's the dividing line. The whole universe is dissolving, I'm told. Isn't that what they call the law of entropy? Everything is breaking down—dispersing—is that right?"

She said, "You're a bit out of my depth. I think it's a bit out of yours, too, isn't it?"

He told her, "You're the one with the master's degree in physics. I barely got through high school science with my head intact. I'm asking you if the law of entropy is valid."

"If it isn't," she replied, smiling, "then all of twentieth century science is built on illusion."

"What is the first law of life?" he asked.

She was still smiling. "This is getting us nowhere. You're trying to enmesh me in doubletalk."

A moment later, he asked her, "If everything is breaking down and dissolving, what builds the flea and the flower? Wouldn't that be the first law?"

"I suppose. I really don't know."

"So what builds life in a dissolving universe? What builds the flea and the flower?"

"Same thing that builds the man, I guess," she replied quietly. "It's not doubletalk. I'm sorry."

"What are we talking about?" he murmured.

"Sanctity of life, I guess."

He said, "I think—April, if anything is sacred about life, then it has to begin right there—with the reversal of the law of entropy. This life force is a counterforce. It builds.

Constructs. In a universe where everything else is falling apart."

She said, very quietly, "Yes. I guess that's true."

"So it's the force itself that is sacred. Not elephants and fleas, men and mice."

"So?"

"So there are corruptions in the translation from force to form. Form is not necessarily sacred, whether we're thinking of fleas or men. The form is not sacred. Depends on what it does . . . and maybe *why* it does."

"Maybe so," she agreed, in a voice once again going distant. "But I think we've missed the whole point of—"

"What is the point?" he said. "The flea represents a successful construction of biological form in a dissolving universe. It is life bottled up and holding together, maintaining, while all around it falls apart. But for only a little while. Soon—especially soon in the case of a flea—entropy finally overcomes that fragile bottle and the flea returns to the dissolving universe."

She was giving him an odd look. "That seems to be true, yes."

"So what's the point?" he asked.

"Answer that," she told him, "and I'll get you an honorary degree at the university of your choice. This has gotten away from us, Mack. What the *hell* are we talking about?"

He gave a tired sigh as he told her, "We're talking about warfare, April. You think it stinks. All the time. Okay, so do I. But I say

70

also that it has its place in whatever scheme is moving this old universe. It could just be that a touch of warfare—appropriately applied here and there—is what sanctifies the whole endeavor. Men and women are not sacred. The things they do, maybe—but there's no sanctity in a bottle of energy."

She said, "That's what we are, huh? Bottles of energy?"

"Until we step outside the bottle, sure."

"Oh, dear me. We are getting, I believe, into *sanctimony*."

He gave her a fish eye as he replied, "That's where we started, dear."

"No, I said—oh, okay, score one for the soldier. What about peace and love, General?"

"Sergeant," he corrected her. "Generals are soldiers of the abstract. Sergeants are soldiers of the specific."

"I stand corrected."

She was getting nasty, again. He said, "What about peace and love? Noble concepts. But illusions of the human mind, I'm afraid, fleeting constructions in a dissolving universe, a misdirection of the creative force that is constantly at war with the entropic tug."

"I can't believe that you really think that. Or that you would *say* it, anyway."

He said, "I believe it and I said it. Peace as an abstract is laziness and defeat. It's the human mind's counterpart for entropy. Its only goal is death because death is the final peace. We even call it that when we try to rationalize some meaning into death."

71

"And what is love?" she snapped.

"In the abstract or in the specific?"

"Let's take the abstract first."

"Fear."

"What?"

"Love in the abstract is fear. It's a veiled recognition that everything I've been saying is true. It's the fear of loneliness, of total isolation, in a crumbling universe—a subconscious doubt that anything is sacred."

She said, "Bunk!"

"You give lip service to brotherly love because it reassures you that you're not really alone," he told her.

"I resent that! I do not give lip service! I think I can truly state that I love all mankind!"

"It's easy to say. But how many *people* do you love?"

"I thought we were talking about the abstract form of love!"

"We are. So, say it's not lip service. Tell me, then, lover—how do you sleep at night?"

"What do you mean?"

"So many of those you abstractly love are in agony right now, April. There are fiends afoot, and not all of those are human. The fiends of hunger, disease, of ignorance and superstition, of natural calamities. How dare you, young lady, pamper yourself through six years of public education while all around you loved ones are in agony. Why the hell weren't you out there feeding them, and carrying water, and binding wounds? Who the hell are you kidding, other than yourself? You have no love for mankind."

"I've heard all that before!" she said angrily. "It's pure bunk! I can't prostrate myself with silly grief over something I cannot possibly control. I can't take care of all the . . . the . . . But that doesn't mean that I don't *care*!"

"Uh huh. We're getting to the nitty of this philosophical discussion."

"*Pseudo* philosophy, you mean! I don't see any tassels of learning on your combat rig, soldier!"

"Yeah, that's what I thought," he said quietly. "You've been patronizing the mean old killer boss, haven't you?"

"I shouldn't have said that," she said, softening the voice somewhat. "I'm sorry. But I *don't* think either of us is qualified to lecture on human philosophy."

"Who is?" Bolan replied gently. "The human situation is pretty much in the same condition as it was when the first philosophers began their discourses. It's enough to make you wonder, isn't it, if any of them ever really caught the truth? Philosophy is simply a stretch of the mind—any mind—and my stretch is as valid as any man's who thinks. I'll tell you a battlefield truth, though. I've never seen a soldier in combat who was not stretching his mind to its limits."

"So love is fear, huh?"

"In the abstract, yes. It becomes something else when it gets specific."

73

"What else?"

"You said it a minute ago. It becomes care."

"I see. Well, I'm glad we finally got that straightened out."

He said, "Uh huh. And that inevitably turns into war."

"Oh really!" she exploded.

Bolan went on, quietly and persistently, making a final try. "You think men or women war because they *don't care*? They make war because they cannot tolerate the alternatives to those they love—be it a person or an ideal. A woman sacrifices for her child because she *hates* the thought of that child going hungry. A man *kills* because he cannot accept peril for his family from the marauder. A civilized nation picks up arms because it will not surrender to the savages."

"Oh, fine. Now you're mixing it all—a woman is going to war every time she breastfeeds her child!"

"Damn right. It's love, and it's war. One cannot exist without the other, in one form or another—so long as life exists in a savagely entropic universe. Take it to the basics. Take it to that pathetic tribe in Africa, the one that has surrendered to entropy. Your anthropologists and psychologists are having a field day with that one. Even the family units have disintegrated, babies lying dead in the streets because their mothers would not feed them. Those people aren't making war and they're not making love. They're lying down and dying. Can you tell me why?"

"No. But I suppose you can."

"I think I could, yeah. But why bother? All you're listening with is your mind. And it's not stretched far enough to hear. So let's just forget it. Slow down. You're doing sixty in a thirty mile zone. And right now I don't need a care package from the Columbus cops."

"They're at war, too, huh?"

"Better believe they are. And you better hope they never decide to lie down and die."

"I'm sorry, Mack," she said softly.

"So am I. Forget it."

She pulled the cruiser into the parking lot at the Holiday Inn. "Am I staying with you?"

"No. I'll meet you in Indianapolis. By midnight."

She recognized the finality of that. "You're all heart, aren't you, Mr. Battlefield Philosopher?"

The young lady was closer to the secret of Mack Bolan than she could realize. But it would require someone other than Bolan to tell her that. He was a lot better at showing than telling.

And the first day of the second mile was already half gone.

CHAPTER 7

LADY'S CHOICE

The motel occupied a low ridge overlooking the Salt Creek Valley, a narrow meadowland stretching a quarter-mile or so between the highway and the higher ridges to the south. Directly opposite the Ramada Inn, a small shopping center had displaced a chunk of that meadow. People in Nashville obviously leaned toward the rustic motif. The entire shopping center and even a fast-foods chain restaurant with national identification appeared to have been built from barn wood. The motel itself looked like no Ramada in Bolan's memory. It was snuggled into the hillside in such a way that it hardly broke the symmetry of the terrain. Dark wood, stone, and smoked glass combined to suggest modern luxury at no expense to rustic charm.

Bolan drove on past the ascending motel

driveway, continuing westerly toward the village. There were schools to the right, another large country inn to the left, then a blinker-light junction with the north-south highway 135—the east-west route doglegging across Salt Creek and climbing into the hills toward Bloomington, the village of Nashville sprawling off to the right and gradually ascending the northward elevations.

Harry the Ape had not been pulling any legs. The tiny town was choked with humanity. Narrow streets and narrower sidewalks were strained far beyond their capacity to carry the foot and motor traffic as visitors flowed in great masses everywhere like so many ants at a picnic spread.

Except for that, it appeared to be a charming little town, yeah—a page from the nation's frontier past. Maybe four blocks square, with many ancient buildings wearing brave faces and here and there a new building wearing a cosmetically ancient face.

The warwagon joined the parade of motor traffic along the main route into town, blending with comfortable anonymity into the line of autos, motorcycles, and recreational vehicles. And Bolan knew that there would be no combat stretch here. Already his mind was beginning to disengage from the idea of a hot clash in this area. The whole valley was choked with human activity. Tour buses, yeah—chalk up another for Harry the Talking Head— chartered Greyhounds and others from far and wide were backed off and parked wherever

77

space could be found. There were sidewalk artists and curbside vendors, shops with colorful names and craftsmen with artistic handiwares; and everywhere people, old and young, flocking in quest of God knew what.

It was a bum go. A traffic light two blocks up the street had been deactivated and a couple of uniformed cops were trying to move the traffic, which was pressing in from four directions.

Bolan had seen enough. He was scouting, not sightseeing, and the results were in. He peeled off at the first cross street and headed back east only to run smack into the high school. A drive there curved along a low hill to move him northward and bring him to high ground at the east edge of the village center. Another east-west roadway presented itself there, flanked by a volunteer fire station and an art gallery. Foot traffic here was thinner but buses were parked all along the roadway and a steady stream of vehicles told the tale of another choked throughway.

He pulled onto the parking apron at the fire station, inspiring a harried looking guy in civilian dress to rush over and bang on his window. "You can't park here!" the guy yelled. "You're blocking the fire station!"

Bolan opened the window and told that guy, "Who's parking? Anyway, you better pray you don't get a fire call. A Sherman tank couldn't get through this town right now."

The guy grinned at him. Bolan had obviously touched a sympathetic nerve. "That's what I been trying to tell the council. We got no fire lanes. The whole damn town could burn down and we'd have to sit here and watch it. But I still can't let you park here, good buddy."

Bolan replied, "I'm trying to get back to the Ramada. How would you do that?"

The guy pointed east as he said, "Just get in line. It'll thin out when you get past the fairgrounds. Do you know where you're at right now?"

Bolan smiled and shook his head.

"Well this's old 46—the old highway. Most of these people are headed to the fairground parking. That's just at the bottom of the hill. You go on past there to just where you start uphill again. Take that right, there. It'll pull you right up into the Ramada the back way. Hey! Just get in behind the choo-choo! That's where he's going."

The guy spun away, stepped into the street, and held up a hand to halt the eastward flow, then hand-signalled Bolan into the line behind a sightseeing "train"—a rubbertired street vehicle disguised as a locomotive and pulling several open cars loaded with passengers.

Bolan tossed the guy a restrained salute and took his place in the outward flow. Several hundred yards and ten minutes later he was past the bottleneck and moving slowly, but continuously, in the wake of the mock train.

It was a few minutes past two o'clock when he pulled up at the Ramada Inn. The congestion here was little better than elsewhere, but he found a place to leave the big rig while he went inside for a quick look.

He'd changed into a $500 set of threads, provided by the finest of Mafia tailors—but he would have felt just as comfortable here in dungarees. It was sheer country charm, yeah—and there was nothing snythetic about it. The good atmosphere was created by heavy wood and native stone, open-beam ceilings, spacious comfort, and a down-home feeling.

Two little girls were playing jacks just inside the lobby. The desk clerks wore Levis; one was neatly bearded. A dozen or so guests idled there in pleasant conversation. The lounge was dark like most bars, but relieved somewhat by plenty of glass at the far wall. A small bandstand and dance floor were now barren, as was most of the lounge. Inviting sofa tables were spread through several rooms and there was a standard bar with padded stools. A young couple sat at a window table with beers; several guys at the bar were having a good time with the bartender and one of the waitresses.

Homey, yeah—friendly.

He went on to the dining room for a quick look. It was huge, comfortably rustic with a stone fireplace set dead in the center of the big room and large enough to garage a Volkswagen. The dining room was loaded—pretty waitresses scurrying, smug diners stuffing themselves—a sort of merry feeling. Homey and friendly, sure.

It was no place for the likes of Mack Bolan.

But, then, he could not always choose his own hellgrounds. And it had been a long time since there'd been any place he could call home.

But he liked this place . . . and he regretted what had come here. Though Bolan was a New Englander, he knew that this was where America was coming from. This was the heartland. All the more reason, then, perhaps . . .

He returned to the lobby and caught the eye of the bearded clerk. "Are you full?" he asked the guy.

A sympathetic smile. "Unless you're reserved, sir—"

"I'm not," Bolan told him. "Is Mr. Tucker registered?"

"Tucker?" The clerk raised an eyebrow. "Roger Tucker?"

"That's the one."

"Oh, well, if you're with—"

"I'm not," Bolan said. "We have an appointment."

"He'll be in around three, sir. Did you want to go to the hospitality room?"

Not exactly. "I think we're meeting in the bar," Bolan said.

"Oh. Well, he maintains—well no, okay. Mr. Tucker has one of our fireplace suites but if you're meeting him in the lounge . . ."

Bolan did not have to struggle to feign indecision. "Well who's in the suite now?"

"His secretary is there, sir."

"Uh huh. Okay—well, okay—what's the number?"

The guy gave him the room number and

directions. Bolan thanked him and wandered away.

The Toonerville choo-choo was loading outside for the return trip to Nashville. He watched that activity for a moment while weighing a decision then went on to the room.

A pretty blonde woman of perhaps twenty-five answered the knock at the hospitality suite. Not exactly Bolan's type but very attractive if a guy didn't look too deeply into the eyes. She wore silk lounging pajamas with a deep plunge clear to the navel and an expectant look that quickly faded as the caller asked her, "Is he here yet?"

"He who?" she inquired warily.

Bolan ignored that. "You must be Jackie. I'm Frank. He said I should introduce myself."

The woman threw the door open and turned her back on the visitor. He stepped inside and closed the door. She was obviously very miffed.

He said, apologetically, "If I'm intruding on something . . ."

She turned a resigned grimace toward him as she replied to that. "Business always intrudes, doesn't it? It's okay. I'm getting used to it. Help yourself at the bar."

It was a nice layout. A fire laid in the fireplace but not yet lit. Plenty of stretch, with comfort if not luxury. Adjoining bedroom, the door standing ajar.

He moved to the open bedroom door for a casual check of the interior.

"The bar's over here," the lady said, eyeing him curiously. "What'd you say your name is?"

"Frank." He went to the bar and mixed a weak whiskey and water. The girl dropped into a chair and watched him with growing interest. He looked at his watch and said, "Well..."

"You're early," she said. "What time did he tell you?"

"Three o'clock."

"It figures."

"What figures?"

She sighed. "He always schedules me along with everyone else. I'm supposed to sit here and vegetate while he—are you down from Chicago?"

Bolan nodded. "How long since you were there?"

"Too long."

He grinned and shook his head. "Nah. You're better off here. He tells me you're getting to be quite the painter."

She laughed drily at that. "Tell the teacher, will you? Frank who?" She was giving him a closer inspection, now.

He said, "Frank Lambert."

"Changed from what?"

Bolan chuckled. "My momma's name is Lambretta."

She said, "I haven't seen you around."

"Haven't been around," he explained. "Just got in."

"I mean around Chicago."

"Not long there, either. I'm really by way of L.A."

"Oh. I like L.A." She was buying him. "Level with me?"

He said, "Sure. It's a great town."

"I don't mean that. What's happening, Frank? I mean, what is really *happening* around here?"

He smiled and shrugged his shoulders. "Ask the man."

"Ask the Sphinx!" she spat. "I'm asking you. What do you do? You're a contractor, aren't you?" It was not a question.

He told her, "Sure. I'll build anything. What do you need?"

"Wise guy," she said, but not with anger.

"If you know," he said, "why ask?"

"I know things are heating up, here. I just want to know how hot and where. I don't want to get caught in the middle of another stupid war."

"You're cool here," he told her.

"With guys like you coming around all the time?" She shook the pretty head. "We came here for the cool. It was nice, while it lasted. Why can't he leave well enough alone?"

Bolan said, "Doesn't work that way, Jackie. You should know that. Heat follows heat."

She said, "Go sing it on a mountain, Lambretta. Heat isn't happy where it's cool—that's all. Nothing *followed* him here. He brought it all with him—coal by coal. He's just building another Chicago down here. Isn't he? Isn't that what he's doing?"

Bolan-Lambretta muttered, "You better ask the man."

"I ask him nothing," she replied bitterly.

84

She flounced into the bedroom and slammed the door.

Which was fine with Bolan. He began a discreet shakedown of the outer room, but it had revealed no secrets when the girl reappeared moments later. She had changed into a skirt and blouse, purse over the shoulder, broad-brimmed straw hat in hand.

"Leaving?" Bolan asked her.

"Watch me," she said quietly.

"What do I tell Carmine?"

"Tell him he knows where to find me," she told the supposed visitor from Chicago.

Bolan blocked her forward progress with an arm across the soft chest. "Tell me so we'll all know," he said softly.

"Go to hell," she said, matching his tone.

"I need to know where you're going, Jackie."

"Why?"

He said, "Maybe it's a personal interest."

"Meaning exactly what?"

"Meaning maybe life or death," he said, with a sober wink.

"You're serious, aren't you?"

"My line of work, kid, is always serious. But it can be fun, too, if certain people are willing."

"What makes you think I might be willing?"

"I never schedule a lady with my business appointments, Jackie."

"Go to hell you bastard you," she whispered. "Where the hell did you get—you're crazy, do you know that? Carmine would skin you alive and hang your hide out to dry."

85

He said, "Maybe it would be worth it. Would it?"

She said, "I guess you'll never know."

He sighed heavily and told her, "Not if I don't know where it is."

An undecided smile was working at those pouting lips. She said, "It would serve him—okay, I'm on 135 north. Left side, you'll see it. The sign reads *Buttons and Bows*."

"What kind of sign?"

"People around here name their houses. That's the name of mine. Just turn down the lane where you see the sign."

He said, "Okay. I'll find you."

She said, "I take it that *he* won't, then."

He told her, "Things are a bit hectic, right now. Maybe he won't be able to."

"And that's why you will."

"Uh huh."

"Tell me what's going on."

"I'll tell you later."

"Something is really wrong, isn't it?"

He said, "I guess it is."

"And you have a personal interest?"

"Uh huh."

"Are you the cure or the kill?" she asked soberly.

"Both," he replied. "Does that worry you?"

"Not a damn bit." She went on to the door, then turned back for a parting shot. "It's worth it, Lambrttta. But bring plenty of balls with you. You're going to need them."

"They follow me everywhere," he quietly assured her.

86

"We'll see about that," she said, departing with soft laughter.

"Like hell we will," Bolan muttered to the empty room.

He gave the lady plenty of time then took his own departure. The time was thirty minutes past the hour of two—and he was playing the ear.

It was no place for a shootout, no.

But if he could just get an eyeball on the guy. . . .

Something caught his attention through the swinging door of the lounge as he strode past, rooting him momentarily in his tracks, then drawing him magnetically back for another look.

But, yeah, the first look was look enough.

At a table, by the window, sat a lady with an exotic drink. She wore a sexy silk chemise and was displaying leg enough to root any man to his tracks.

She was, yeah, a lady fed.

With a dumb name like April Rose.

CHAPTER 8

MESSAGES

Bolan slid in beside the lady and quietly asked, "Taking the scenic route to Indy?"

April Rose showed him a sober smile as she replied, "Sorry, soldier, you were countermanded. Has your man shown up yet?"

He said, "Not yet. But I'm expecting his forward scouts at any moment. So let's make this quick. What countermand?"

"I called Mr. Brognola to report the developments. He was, uh, thrilled to hear from me. Been trying to reach you since early morning. Uh, what's a floater?"

"Mobile phone in the cruiser," Bolan explained. "Automatic answering and recording system."

"He says you should turn it on and collect your messages. He's been leaving one every hour since nine o'clock."

The waitress had arrived to take Bolan's order. He sent her after a screwdriver, then asked his lovely companion, "What's the message?"

April was busy checking out his attire. "You're beautiful," she said, "in a gangsterish sort of way. Is that the idea?"

"Uh huh. What's the message?"

"Something big is brewing in Indiana."

Bolan frowned and replied, "Tell him I said thanks for the message but I'm several jumps ahead of it. Now you—"

"There's more. But, first, you and I have to find an understanding."

"We found it," he told her, lightly. "There's likely to be a pile of sacred blood spilled around here, and very shortly. Message or no, I want that noble body of yours to hell and gone out of here on the double-damn-quick."

Her eyes were glowing. "Uh huh. He said that was the real problem."

"What?"

"Mr. Brognola. He told me about . . . all the friends you've lost, uh, that you've lost. That you were just concerned for my safety."

Sure he was concerned. But it went a bit farther than that, too. And Bolan could not tell this lovely lady that she was poison to him—a double hazard to his survival all the time she remained in his shadow.

Instead, he said, "Okay, so I worry. With very good reason. But that's not the all of it. There are fighters and there are lovers, April. I read you as a lover. It's just—"

"It's just baloney," she said sweetly. "You told me that war and love are one and the same. If I'm a lover than I must also be a warrior. And if *you* are a warrior . . ."

Bolan had to smile. She'd turned it back on him. Nor had he been entirely truthful with her—he was expecting no bloodshed in the immediate moments ahead. He said, "Have I told you how very lovely you are?"

It took her totally by surprise. And it flustered her. Their eyes locked for a moment, then she bent quickly to her drink to cover the confusion. A moment later she murmured, "No, you hadn't."

He said, "Well . . . I noticed."

"Thanks for telling me."

"Don't mention it."

"Are you?"

"Am I what?"

"A lover?"

Bolan was trying to keep it light. He screwed his face into a thoughtful grimace as he told her, "Let's leave the question open for now."

The lady was very solemn. "Mr. Brognola says you are. He said that hate could never have brought you this far."

"What else did he tell you? What's that message?"

"Am I staying?" she asked soberly.

"You can finish your drink, yeah."

"Gee, thanks. You're a peach."

"We're running out of time, April," he said, with genuine regret. "What's the message?"

90

But they had already run out of time.

Tuscanotte's chief headhunter, Fuzz Martin, stepped into the lounge and went straight to the bar. The first eye the guy caught was Bolan's. Something flickered and danced briefly in that clash of eyes before the Martin gaze moved on to April Rose and then to a quick scan of the other patrons.

Martin was a former sergeant of detectives with the Chicago police. He'd been busted off the force some ten years back—some said because he wouldn't share his mob envelopes with a superior—and had been in Tuscanotte's personal cadre ever since. He was a big beefy guy with purple veins in his nose and maybe a touch of insanity in the eyes. It had been widely reported that he delighted in breaking bones and wallowing in other men's blood. Bolan had an electronic file on the guy twenty-eight lines long and he could have added another thirty to the computer's data bank if he'd wished to clutter it with ghoulish repetition.

A touch of madness, yeah—but insane did not mean dumb.

The guy was in and out of there in a flash. April Rose had not even noticed him. She was beginning to relate the long delayed message from Brognola when Bolan put a hand on hers and said, "Save it. Get up right now and go to the lady's room. Don't delay and don't look back. Just go."

Her eyes were seeking an explanation but Bolan was already up and moving. He went

91

around the partition to the dining room and caught a glimpse of Willie Frio as the number two tagman darted past the cashier's station in a quick withdrawal along the hall toward the lobby.

That hallway also served the main entrance to the lounge.

Bolan was moving swiftly, with single-minded purpose, but Frio was rounding the corner into the lobby as Bolan gained the cashier's station.

That main hall traveled east-west, between lobby and dining room. A short north-south passageway struck off just above the dining room and carried toward the north side of the building—the entrance side.

Bolan followed his instincts and turned into the short hall just as April Rose came through the doorway from the lounge.

His irritation with that circumstance quickly melted as he realized that she was following instructions; the short hall led to the rest rooms. But it also served an entrance to the motel offices, and he reached that point at the same moment that Martin and Frio were exiting from the lobby.

He had them in perfect view via the glass wall of the office and an outside window—and he had Tuscanotte framed there, as well.

The Mafia boss was standing beside a burgundy Continental town sedan with the passenger door open. Apparently he had just stepped out of the vehicle. Frio was trying to push him back inside. An argument was going down, with Fuzz Martin quickly joining in.

A perfumed presence moved in behind Bolan and April Rose's breathless voice whispered in his ear. "Is that him?"

"The little guy, yeah," Bolan replied. "I blew it. His headhunters spotted me."

"Do they know you?"

"Don't have to," he explained. "All they saw was a possible threat. It's all they were looking for."

"Well, what a terrible way to live! So what?"

He gave her a gentle shove and growled. "Back to the table—quick!"

Tuscanotte was coming in anyway. The super cautious tagmen had lost the argument.

And April Rose was giving none whatever. She moved quickly along the hallway without a murmur.

Bolan moved on past the offices, through a cloak room, and into the lobby. It put him right at the front door. And he was standing there when Carmine Tuscanotte stepped inside.

"Hi, Carmine," he said breezily. "Long time unseen. Come on in and I'll tell you why you sent for me."

CHAPTER 9

STRETCHING

In earlier times, the guy would have never amounted to anything more than a third rate neighborhood boss—and even that level of power had been handed to him through bloodlines via the late Jake Vecci. At the time of Bolan's purge of the Chicago power trust, Tuscanotte was not even on his hit list. But the wheel of fortune had spun quickly and dramatically for the smalltimer from the suburbs, once the real power structure of Chicago had been dismantled. And though he was not exactly a visionary, the guy had shown himself to be, at the least, a superb opportunist.

Not so dumb, either.

Dumb never made it big in the underworld. Nor did blind luck. But Carmine Tuscanotte had suddenly emerged as one of the three most likely to succeed to the reins of power in the Chicago Mob. By simple extension, that also could mean boss of the whole damned USA. Chicago was not the only area reeling under the Executioner's persistent assaults. All the Mobs everywhere were now in disarray. But none were down for the full count. One of them, somewhere—if left to its own devices— would find the right combination for a true power structure to replace the old.

Bolan was reading the Chicago Outfit as the most likely to succeed in that endeavor. Which is why he had picked them as Monday's Mob.

And now he was shaking hands with the emerging boss of that Mob. It seemed the only thing left to do, considering the circumstances.

The lobby was still crowded with guests. The two little girls still played near the entrance. The sightseer choo-choo was making another arrival.

Tuscanotte was giving him a shrewd appraisal over the handshake. "I don't think I know you, Lambretta."

"Everybody back east knows you, Carmine."

"They do, eh? You mean everybody that's *left* back east."

Bolan-Lambretta chuckled soberly as he replied to that. "So things are tough all over. How 'bout you?"

"We're getting by."

Bolan's gaze deliberately swept the lobby. He said, "So I see."

The guy laughed a little at that. "I said, getting by. How'd you find it?"

"Ben Davis sent me."

There was no change of expression as the *Mafioso* asked, "Why?"

"He got hit this morning."

"What d'ya mean, *hit*?"

Bolan spelled it for him, adding, "The whole damn operation went up in flames. All the product—everything. Somebody torched it. Ben thought you'd want to know. He's, uh, indisposed at the moment."

"Let's go to the bar," Tuscanotte said quickly.

That was fine with Bolan. He was playing the ear, accepting whatever could come from the busted play. The two bodyguards were staying loose, watching him from a distance.

Tuscanotte exchanged pleasant greetings with various motel employees as they threaded their way through the lobby. The guy was obviously well known and respected as "Mr. Tucker." A barmaid tossed him a cheery hello, also, as they entered the lounge.

Willie Frio had gone on ahead and was taking a seat in one of the back rooms.

The renegade cop stood casually at the check-in desk in the lobby, small-talking with the bearded clerk.

Tuscanotte's eye went instantly and interestedly to April Rose—and Bolan noted that he selected a table that afforded a continuing view of that pleasing sight.

Bolan sat down with his back to the lady.

A waitress was there before they could get settled in, smiling at the genial "Mr. Tucker."

The guy patted her hip and asked, "How's Joe?"

"Joe's fine," she replied. "Where've you been drinking lately?"

"Business trip," Tuscanotte replied, making an unhappy face. "No place like home, eh? Bring me the usual, Jenny."

The girl asked Bolan, "Shall I bring your screwdriver from the other table?"

"Leave it there," he instructed. "I'll get back to it in a minute."

But it was already a lost effort. the *Mafioso*'s eyes had already scanned across to pick out the screwdriver at the table with the beautiful lady.

"Invite the lady over," he suggested, when the waitress departed.

"We need a few words, first," Bolan told him.

"Okay. But speak softly. What happened down there?"

"I don't know exactly. There was gunfire. Then the whole place went up. Total loss, Carmine."

"Call me Roger, here."

"Sure. But you still lost it all."

"Where do you fit?"

"I was making a buy. We been doing business with you for a long time."

"How'd you know it was me?"

Bolan gave him a knowing grin. "Come on," he said. "We always know."

"You're out of New York?"

97

Bolan nodded an affirmative response to that.

"Who're you with?"

"It used to be Marinello. Poor Augie. God knows who it is, now. Do you?"

Tuscanotte chuckled. "I'm not God."

"The word I hear," Bolan said quietly, "is that you could be . . . if you play it right."

The guy chuckled again. The waitress came with his drink. He exchanged a couple of wisecracks with her then watched her departure before he got back to his visitor. "So Ben sent you to Nashville."

"He sent me to Stoney Gap Hill. The Apeman sent me on here."

"I find that hard to believe."

"Don't believe it, then. But I'm here."

He was a deceptively laid-back guy, full of chuckles and genial smiles. Not a bad looking guy—still hard and lean at forty—maybe even handsome, to some women. But Bolan knew where he was at—and he knew how thin the ice at his feet.

Tuscanotte was smiling at his wristwatch. He turned the same smile toward Bolan-Lambretta as he said, "I'm meeting some people here in a few minutes. Why didn't Harry send himself?"

"You better scrub your meeting. Harry didn't send himself because he wasn't able to. All of your Stoney Lonesome boys are dead."

The guy had iron self-control; Bolan had to give him that. He casually got to his feet, still smiling, and very quietly said to Bolan-Lambretta, "I suddenly remember another appointment. You hang around here and I'll call you back. This is all very interesting and I want to hear more about it when I get time. Hey—I appreciate all the trouble you've gone to, and I'll make it up to you." He sent another flick of the eyes toward April Rose and went out, pausing for an instant at the bar for a friendly word to the bartender.

And Bolan was suddenly very glad that he'd come to Indiana.

Carmine Tuscanotte was no third-rate punk.

The guy was a survivor—and that was the kind who worried Mack Bolan the most.

Willy Frio was nowhere in sight. Apparently there was another way out, beyond the dance floor.

Bolan sat there for a couple of beats, then joined April Rose.

"What happened?" she whispered furiously.

"I sent him away," Bolan told her.

"But why?"

"To get some stretch."

"To get what?"

There was no time to explain the ground rules of Mack Bolan's war. He asked the lady, "Did the strike force cover it in Louisville?"

She nodded vigorously. "Yes. They closed in right behind us. Why?"

"Because I used a guy's name in vain," he explained. "Carmine will be looking into that. I need to know how far he can look."

She replied, "If you mean can he speak to

99

any of the principals, the answer is no. Not for at least another twenty-four hours."

He said, "Good enough. I'm playing the ear now, April. I don't know where it will take me. My name is Frank Lambretta. Remember it. You stick right here. If a call comes from me or for me, take it and play it."

He was rising for a quick departure when she caught his arm and urgently whispered, "The message from Brognola. It's—"

He said, "It will have to keep," and went quickly out of there, again through the dining room. This time he used the kitchen exit and reached the northwest corner of the building in time to note the leisurely departure of the burgundy-colored Continental.

They were running east, taking the back way out.

And that was okay. It was fine.

So was Bolan—in his war machine—rolling, he hoped, toward some combat stretch.

CHAPTER 10

BEYOND

The target was tracking east on the old high-way—headed, apparently, toward the junction with the bypass route about two miles out of town. And that was a puzzle for the man at the con. He had not expected them to run toward Columbus. Returning immediately to the scene of the reported hit was not exactly standard routine for a guy in Tuscanotte's situation.

But the puzzle was solved a half-mile short of the junction. Bolan was coming down off a high, winding hill and dropping back into the Salt Creek Valley, the target vehicle in plain view several hundred yards ahead. He could see the choked bypass route running parallel to the south along the valley floor and converging for the meet at some unseen point ahead. Coming in along the north flank was another converging road, joining the old highway at the bottom of the hill at a very close angle to form a vee. It was a gravelled, narrow road with a broad turnout. Several vehicles were parked there, their snouts pointing into the northwest.

The burgundy Continental took the 150-degree left turn and halted beside the parked vehicles. Doors sprang open all along that line and guys were scrambling out for an obvious roadside parley.

Bolan drove slowly by, the optic scans at full operation. He did not like the looks of that dirt road. Signboards at the junction proclaimed the existence, somewhere along that road, of Camp Palawopec—"For Boys and Girls"—and also a CYO Camp called Rancho Framasa. That seemed innocent enough, sure—but the roadway itself ran along the base of a steep, wooded ridge and became almost instantly swallowed by overhanging trees. A rushing creek, fed by recent rains, tumbled along at the other side of the narrow roadway. It would not be a comforting route on which to go a'venturing.

He proceeded on for another several hundred yards to a point where the old highway took a sudden 90-degree jog around that same ridge and found there a place to pull off and take stock.

The video recorder was showing fourteen seconds in the collector. The slow-mo replay showed quite a bit more than that. And it indicated that Harry the survivor Venturi had

102

kept out a card or two in his survival show-down.

Without further ado, Bolan plugged in his radiophone and played a card of his own. "This is Striker," he told the familiar, responding voice at the funny phone 800 miles away. "I'm on the floater so be guided."

"I was about to give you up, Striker," said the old friend. "What's your present situation?"

"Not too happy," Bolan admitted. "You'll remember the living legends of a day or so ago. I'm near the little town of the same name. And I just found a couple of surprises. Living legends of a different type. Is that why all the flags on my floater?"

"That's why, yeah," Brognola told him. "We intercepted some rather revealing, uh, communications this morning. I hate to say it but it appears that you've stumbled into, uh, no man's land. A veritable, uh, Shangri-la for those living legends of the other type."

Bolan thoughtfully replied, "Yeah, okay— that's the reading I'm getting at present place. I just wanted it confirmed. Where'd you get yours? Chicago?"

"Uh huh. Can you call me on a laundry line?"

"Not right at the moment, no," Bolan replied, sighing. "I have the tiger by its tail and I hate like hell to let go. It could drag me any-where and I don't much like the looks of this jungle. But if I let go . . . well, I've got this time problem, you know. This could be the golden opportunity."

"It could be the land of the beyond, too, buddy," Brognola said heavily. "Our figures indicate an overwhelming superiority on the other side. And that's not Miami Beach, you know. Frankly I don't see much comfort for you there."

"I'll just have to clear a comfort zone, then," Bolan said. "Are you reading another Miami Beach?"

"On a regional scale, yeah."

"How much region are we talking about?"

"You're in it, pal," Brognola replied, with a sober laugh. "We're talking about all of it."

"The heartland," Bolan muttered.

"You've got it."

Bolan sighed into the radiophone hookup and lit a cigarette.

Presently, Brognola said, "Striker?"

"I'm still here."

"What are you skulling?"

"The golden opportunity."

"Don't try it. That's my friendly advice. I can't move into that area without tipping everything. About the best I can offer is after the fact. And that could be damn little comfort for you, pal."

Bolan said, very quietly, "I know."

"We don't think it's worth it, Striker."

"Then nothing's worth it," Bolan replied tiredly. "This is the very thing I—hell, I can't let them have it. It's the Monday coalition, Hal. If they make it here, then all of the past has been in vain. All the sanctified past, buddy. I cannot give them that."

Brognola knew it. The long, resigned sigh from 800 miles out told it all. "Well . . . maybe we *were* a bit premature with the happy prognosis. This not the same ballgame we discussed in Derby Town, you know. Not at all. Let me suggest a, uh, review of the situation. I don't think we should—"

"It's a go, Hal."

"Uh, well, okay . . . no one can make that decision but you. But I still think . . ."

"Contact the lady helper, will you. You should find her in the lounge at the Ramada, present place. Order her on to Indy. That's a no-fail, Hal."

"No-fail, okay. Keep me posted, dammit— will you? And here's a local clue for you. Divine Light."

"Come back?"

"With a capital D and a capital L. Divine Light. Sorry, that's all I have. But look for it."

Bolan chuckled solemnly and assured his friend in Wonderland that he would look for that.

Then he terminated the contact and turned back to present place.

One of the vehicles that had been parked at the dirt road turnout had peeled about onto the blacktop and was advancing on him at a high rate of speed.

He backed the cruiser into the driveway of a farmhouse and locked the optics onto that approaching vehicle, then energized the fire control system.

The roof-mounted rocket pod quivered in her concealed nest below the sliding panel, awaiting the command to rise and lock.

But that command was not necessary. The speeding vehicle hardly slowed for the 90-degree curve, roaring on past the cruiser with quickening acceleration.

That was a gun crew in there.

A scouting party, maybe. Bound for Stoney Lonesome, perhaps, to verify a reported hit in the home grounds.

The other vehicles in that column at the vee junction were now rolling on, proceeding along the gravelled road toward the camps for boys and girls.

And there was, Bolan suspected, more than camps for boys and girls along that twisted road to nowhere. There was also an encampment of another kind, maybe—a Shangrila?—where all the disputatious hoods of Monday's Mob were coming together in conference assembled. Seeking the Divine Light?

It was, yeah, a golden opportunity.

But yes, Hal, it could also very well become the land of the beyond for Mack Bolan.

But, then, that was the land of the Executioner's birth—wasn't it? It was where he had lived throughout all that sanctified past.

So how about it, April Rose? What could the pretty lady possibly know about it? Mack Bolan had known a lot of sacred lives. And he'd met them each and every one in Hell.

It had a name—Clay Lick Road—and it served a narrow, sparsely settled and rolling valley that had probably been formed in ages past by what was now the creek or "lick." Bolan had noted that the hills in this area seemed to be succession of finger ridges, oriented generally toward an east-west lie. Some were quite high and steep; others lifted gradually into elevated slopes or rolled gently away at bisecting angles. Moraines, perhaps, left by the recession of the glaciers at the end of the last ice age. Whatever—it was rugged and beautiful country. And Bolan could understand Venturi's confused "autumn trees" report. Except where small patches had been cleared for farming, the entire countryside was densely wooded with a variety of trees whose autumn leaves would no doubt provide a stunning and spectacular color display. Bolan was no expert on forestry, but he could recognize hickory, walnut, birch, dogwood and laurel in abundance.

The first half-mile or so along Clay Lick was like a tunnel with overhanging trees forming the roof, a steep ridge rising abruptly along the one side and the rain-swollen creek raging along the other.

And there was no comfort here, no, for the man in the warwagon.

But then the creek formed an S-pattern, crossing twice beneath the narrow roadway to form a wider valley with a gently sloping rise leftward. Several neat homes and cultivated fields appeared there—some corn, and another crop that Bolan did not instantly recognize as tobacco. Cows grazed on the higher elevations, just below the timberline.

Clay Lick meandered away in the midst of that pastoral beauty, crossing toward the far side of the valley—a distance of less than a quarter-mile at the broadest point. The road kept its place beside the steep ridge and topped a gentle rise below which evergreen saplings— Christmas trees?—replaced the other crops; and then, quite abruptly and just over another brief rise, the Christmas trees were replaced by Divine Light.

Yeah.

Thanks, Hal—it was quite a clue.

Clay Lick had found its way back to within fifty feet of the roadway. A narrow drive with a broad turnout sprang away to the left to cross the creek and enter parklike grounds, which rose gracefully to forested ridgeland deep within. No structures revealed themselves to casual view; all that showed was a tree-lined drive flanked by acres of well-tended lawn, which was flanked in turn by dense timberland. An earthen mound suggested of a dam appeared to lift the drive in a curving rise to the ridgeland beyond—and Bolan caught a flash through the trees that he read as the column of vehicles disappearing into those depths.

There was no fencing. Apparently none was needed. The surging creek provided a natural barrier. A narrow, concrete bridge designed to allow waterflow across it was chainblocked in a manner similar to the joint on Stoney Hill.

A couple of guys in shirtsleeves were playing catch with a football just inside the grounds. Another rode slowly across the grass on a small motorcycle.

"No Trespassing" signs abounded at the approaches—but the sign most interesting was a handcarved rustic affair of perhaps two feet square that was nailed to a tree—rather immodestly proclaiming in burnt letters *Divine Light Retreat.* ..

Shangri-la, yeah, maybe. And a damn large chunk of it, at that—perhaps hundreds of acres.

It appeared that Monday's Mob had found themselves the perfect joint—a sanctuary, as it were, in the heartland. And Mack Bolan would have to see about that. But it was no place to go a'blundering. He needed, first, their numbers and nameplates—and he needed to know precisely where they were and what they were doing.

There was too much confusion here, at the moment.

Brognola had hinted at an organizational summit meeting, involving all the gangland principals of the Midwest region. On the other hand, Harry Venturi had sworn on his life that Tuscanotte was meeting with a couple of state guys.

Knowing the Mafia mind as he did, Bolan was almost positive that the information from Venturi was solid as far as it went. A guy like

Venturi, in those circumstances, would not risk an out and out lie. He would hedge, postulate, and withhold—but he would not challenge Bolan's instincts for the truth with an outright lie.

So . . . put it together.

There *had* been a three o'clock meeting scheduled at the Ramada with some state officials. And there *was* a congregation of heartland hoods at a place called Divine Light.

So something large was brewing . . . sure.

A simple hit on the person of Carmine Tuscanotte would not be enough to kill the brew . . . not now.

And there was this time problem.

There was only one logical step next in line for Mack Bolan. As disheartening as the thought might be, he had to penetrate that joint. He had to get inside and sort it out.

He had to take that step beyond.

CHAPTER 11

THE SORT

It was nothing but marshy floodplain backed up by impenetrable thickets for the first several hundred yards beyond the entrance to the hardsite. The creek had disappeared, angling off again into the thickets while the road maintained position in the shadow of the ridge. But then suddenly Clay Lick returned to shoot across beneath the roadway and run along the right side, between road and ridge. And it was a godsend. Just beyond that point another driveway came down from a farm house set upon a grassy hillside.

Divine Light—or access to it—probably lay just over that hill, beyond the farmhouse. The terrain display from the navigation computer seemed to verify that. He was at the northeast corner of the hardsite—on the backhill side, if the contour map knew what it was talking about. Which was probably as close as he was likely to get in a vehicle.

The farm looked deserted.

He pulled into the drive and made the approach with optic and audio scans probing— and these confirmed the naked sense impressions: there was no one about. From the looks of things, there had not been for some time.

He took the cruiser on to the rear and parked it behind the house, then went to the light table in the war room and patched the NavCom display for an inch by inch scrutiny of the terrain features. Twenty minutes later he knew the territory like a native.

There was a large lake up there—perhaps covering five to six acres—formed by throwing up a dam across a deep ravine. That explained the earthen mound eyeballed during the cruise by. The lake was oriented almost precisely north-south, long and narrow. The sector map had no way of knowing about water depths, of course, but it had been made after the lake was built and the dam itself was contoured on the map, revealing—with an acceptable margin for error—the approximate surface elevation of the lake. The result was a rugged shoreline with steep banks everywhere except for the final few hundred feet on each shore at the south end—the dam end. Those steep banks were the sides of the ravine in which the lake lay. Ridges, yeah—a half-dozen within easy gunshot of the creek, lying like gnarled fingers upon the land, chaotic contours on the terrain chart.

And that could be good.

Or it could be bad.

No man-made structures showed on the map. There was no way to know what was really up there, without physical penetration. And there was no way to know in advance just how security conscious those people might be.

It was tempting to believe that the land itself would lull them into a false sense of security. They had it all going for them—except against a most determined foe. And Bolan had one small scrap of intelligence working for him. He thought that he had glimpsed the column of cars crossing the dam and climbing the second ridge.

So okay.

He climbed into the Mafia mind and drew a defensive network. What *did* they have working for them? Up front, at the eastern boundary, they had a swollen creek and a single, guarded access to the property. Working back from there, they had several hundred yards of open lawn, a wooded ridge, a dam, a lake, and another very steep wooded ridge upon which—*maybe*—perched the central camp. To the north, west, and south they had chaotic and densely timbered ridgelands. The entire area was a forest, except for a small scoop here and there carved out for isolated human habitation.

It could make a guy from the big city streets feel pretty secure . . . sure.

So okay. Defend it. Put a couple of guys down at the bridge and give them something to play with so they wouldn't look too obvious to casual passersby. Give another guy a trailbike and let him patrol the creek from the inside. And maybe, just maybe, a silent sentry at each corner of the property ilne. For double safe, another trailbike to patrol the ridges. That would do it up brown. The land itself would do the rest.

Okay.

Bolan went aft and again changed clothing. He got into army camouflage fatigues and combat boots, strapped on a web belt with ammo pouches for the big Weatherby, added the Beretta shoulder rig and affixed the silencer, draped binoculars from the neck, thought twice and decided on the long stiletto and a couple of nylon garrotes. Then he quickly fieldstripped the Weatherby Mark V and made her shiny clean in all her parts, put in a load of .460 bonebusters, shoulder-slung the heavy weapon, and went EVA.

Several minutes later he had to score a point for the streetcorner soldiers from Chicago. They had a sentry at the northeast corner. But the guy must have thought the bosses were crazy. He was taking a sun bath, stripped to the waist and sprawling on a claybank in the open, staring into the western sky with a hand shading his eyes. A neglected shotgun lay beside him.

It was cleared ground—though long neglected and growing kneehigh grass wherever it would grow—where evidently some years earlier evergreen saplings had been planted to

114

grow into God's own Christmas trees. But the crop had never been harvested. Mature Scotch pines now stood in choked rows along the ridgeline—and at the edge of the cleared area a savage from Chicago lay basking in the same radiant energy that made the pines grow.

Bolan came out of tall grass and vaulted rusted barbed-wire to penetrate the enemy turf.

The guy came up quickly and snatched at the shotgun as he whirled to confront the interloper. "You're trespassing, dummy," he snarled, perhaps more angry at being startled than anything else. "You can't hunt here!"

Bolan said, "Do tell," as he pulled two pounds on the Beretta once from the hip. The black pistol sneezed softly and the guy swallowed his snarl—lips, teeth, chin and all.

Bolan seized a foot and dragged the remains into the pines. A wallet identified the guy as Edward Kramer. He was not a brother of the blood but a one-time freelancer who'd made Bolan's personnel file under various sponsors. Not exactly a reliable type—and that confirmed a growing feeling that the Chicago Outfit was relying more and more on mercenaries from outside the bloodlines, an indication that the manpower problem was getting serious.

He went back and scuffed the earth with a foot to cover the bloodstains, then stashed the clothing and shotgun near the body and went quickly on.

There was a lot of ground yet to be covered. And he had to cover it all before contemplating any open assault. Bloodless mercenaries or not, it was no place to go a'blundering.

Ten minutes later, he knew that he was in for a hell of a fight.

He was seated at the top of a sheer rock bluff near the north end of the lake, studying the lie with binoculars. Two large houses stood upon the west bank, at the south end near the dam. Another smaller house was set back away from the east bank, on much lower ground but commanding the access drive at the point where it met the dam.

The west bank, below the larger of the two houses, was entertaining a large number of people. There was about an acre of terraced lawn there, sweeping gracefully down from the house to the lakeside where a small pier provided tie-ups for several rowboats. A rack of canoes stood at the shoreline twenty feet or so north of the pier.

Shangri-la for sure, but most of those guys did not seem to know what to do with it. Many wore business suits—coat, tie, the whole bit. A couple in shirtsleeves stood on the pier, staring vacantly at the lake. A few had ventured onto the water, via a pontoon barge with a canvas awning; one of these was playing with a fishing rod.

While Bolan was studying that situation, a vehicle appeared suddenly at the east side and swung onto the dam, paused there for a moment, then went on across and disappeared as it climbed through the trees of the west bank.

A hell of a fight, yes.

He had caught only a quick glimpse into the interior of that vehicle but it was glimpse enough with no possibility of mistaken impression. It carried four persons—two in the front seat and two in the rear.

The guy on the passenger side up front was sometimes called, by his brothers, the Apeman.

Seated directly behind Venturi was a woman—a very pretty and frightened young woman.

And that was, sure, none other than April Rose.

No further sorting of the characters at Divine Light was necessary.

Bolan knew, now, that all sorts would fall out the same. The only questions remaining were those of time . . . and combat capability.

And all the educated answers were entirely dismal . . . for the pretty lady who loved all mankind.

CHAPTER 12

COCK O' THE ROOST

Venturi was scared as hell. He'd never seen this joint before or even dreamed of its existence. But it was very obvious what it was. And he just couldn't believe it. How long had Carmine been double-dealing him this way?

Shouldn't the head cock, by God, know about a joint like this on his own turf?

Willy Frio pulled hard on the wheel and sent the car careening into seemingly open air. But it was not open air. It was a narrow roadway with room for one-way traffic only—a straight plunge for about fifty feet off to the left, a goddam lake lapping at the other side just a few feet away.

And it made Venturi feel more nervous than ever. Large bodies of water had a way of affecting him in that manner. He'd helped prepare too many cement coffins to ever feel easy around water when things seemed to not be going well.

Frio had paused to give him a look. "Nice, huh?" the wheelman said, inviting comment.

"How deep is it?" Venturi inquired nervously.

"We ain't found the bottom yet, in places. And it's dark down there, man, really murky. The bottom is black mud, yucky muck. I bet almost anything would bury itself if it ever got down there. We dropped an anchor the other day and had to end up cutting the damn rope. Couldn't pull the anchor out of the muck. Forms a vacuum, see. Just sucks it right down."

Venturi shivered and said, "Yeah."

"'Sfunny, it looks real clear up at the top. Like spring water. But I guess it's all the crap at the bottom that yucks it up."

"Cut the yuck and go on," Fuzz Martin growled from the back seat.

Willy eased the car on across the dam. A lot of guys were out. Venturi recognized some of them, sure—but not many. So what the hell was it all about?

It was some joint, for sure. Big house on the hill with two levels, stone and wood with plenty of glass—apparently a screened porch clear across the upper level, a lot of lawn with umbrella tables scattered about. Just beyond the big joint, a two-story A-frame snuggled into the hillside with nothing but glass in front. Nice, yeah. But for what?

They climbed a steep hill and took another

119

abrupt turn at the top. The driveway circled out from that point, encompassing another large oval of lawn and passing to the rear of the A-frame before returning to the main house. Woods, woods everywhere. Venturi was learning to hate trees with a passion.

"Home sweet home," Willy Frio muttered. "If you don't see the light here, Harry, you never will." He chuckled at his joke. "None of us will, I guess. Boss says it's now or never."

"He should've told me," Venturi grumbled. "The head cock ought to know—"

"Hell we just saw it ourselves for the first time last week," the wheelman explained. "He didn't want to take no chance on—"

"Knock it off," came the warning from the rear. "We got big ears back here."

Frio winked at Venturi and pulled the car into a parking space between the houses. Fuzz Martin hustled the broad out and hurried her into the big joint.

Venturi sighed and asked, "Who's the ball-buster?"

"You don't know?" Frio replied with a bit of surprise.

"No I don't know. I asked, didn't I?"

Frio sighed and said nothing.

Venturi opened his door and stuck a leg out, then lit a cigarette and turned back to the wheelman. "Who, uh, who's all here, Willy?"

Frio's eyes were dancing as he replied, "Hell, everybody's here." He laughed. "The gang's all here. Natty Scarbo. Paul Reina. Gummo Gulacci." He paused for dramatic effect. "And all their boys. It's a full table, Harry."

Venturi was beginning to think like a head cock for the first time in a long time. "How many boys have *we* got here?"

"They're *all* here, Harry."

"Since when?"

"Since about noon today."

"All the boys from Cicero?"

"Sure."

"Elmhurst?"

"Them too."

"Who the hell is mindin' the store?"

Frio got out of the car laughing. He said, "Carmine is prob'ly waiting to see you. You better go on in."

"What'd you tell him, Willy?"

"About what? Isn't this a beautiful joint? You can *breathe* up here, man. And wait'll it gets dark. You never heard such noises come outta these woods. Man, it is outta sight. You'll be bunking in the A-frame, so you'll get it all. The big joint, now, is—"

"I need to know what you told 'em, Willy."

"Hey. I told 'im exactly what you told me. You got hit. You were cooling. What's to tell? Take a friendly tip, Harry. You go in there and talk to the man with plain truth in your teeth. Don't be asking me nothing."

Venturi sighed, squared his shoulders, and entered the house. A kitchen went off to the right, just inside. Joe Torrio out of Hammond thrust a cold beer at him as he went past but Venturi waved it away and crossed a small

121

foyer to a large, open room with shoetop-deep blue carpet, open-beam cathedral ceiling, huge stone fireplace at one wall, sliding glass doors covering the whole front.

Two jittery looking strangers sat alone in a far corner watching a ballgame on TV. They were obviously not company men and looked very much out of place.

The glass doors at the front wall were all open. Ten or twelve guys sat out there on the screened veranda with beers and quiet small talk.

The only one he recognized right off was Bebe Frazelli, a lieutenant under Scarbo. Bebe turned to him with a pleased smile and said, "Well, hell! Hi, Harry. Long time."

"Too long, Mr. Frazelli," Venturi replied. "You enjoying the country air?"

"Maybe I'll get used to it," the Bebe said, chuckling.

"I'm looking for Carmine," Venturi told him.

Frazelli jerked his head toward the outside. "Downstairs on the patio. Maybe you should wait."

"Why?"

The junior ranker rolled his eyes and said, "I think he just found a new playmate. Second thought, maybe you should go down. Maybe you can talk him into passing her around."

Venturi forced a laugh and went down the stairs to the lower level. It was one of those joints where both floors touch the ground. It was built into the hillside, with the top level grounding at the rear, the lower at the front. Down there was another lounge area and more glass wall opening onto an oval shaped patio.

Twenty feet or so of lawn extended on from the patio to complete that level; from that point, the lawn sloped several hundred feet down to the lake.

Carmine was at a patio table with Scarbo and Reina. Gulacci was walking slowly along the grassy slope toward the lake. The broad sat between Carmine and Reina. Scarbo, across the table, was licking her with his eyes. Some guy whom Venturi did not recognize was placing a coke in front of the broad. Fuzz Martin stood off to the side—the perfect bodyboss—listening while not listening, watching while not watching.

Carmine looked up and noted Venturi's presence but did not acknowledge it by word or deed. He was, for sure, very much interested in that broad.

Venturi went over to stand in Fuzz Martin's shadow.

Carmine was talking to the broad. She was scared—really scared—and it showed very plainly.

"What'd you say your name was, honey?"

"I said it was April Rose and it still is. What's yours?"

Carmine chuckled. He knew, too, how scared she was and he was enjoying it. "That's not the name of a *person*," he said amiably.

"It's the name of this person," the scared broad insisted.

"Changed from what? Roseberg? Rosenstein?"

"Maybe," she said quietly. Even scared to death, the baby had a touch of class. But for how long?

Carmine was playing her. "There's no maybe, honey. It is or it isn't. So what is it?"

She took a shuddering breath and told him, "My daddy's name is Rose. His daddy's name was Rose. It's a valid name. If you don't like it, change it."

Carmine poked Reina with an elbow and said, "I'd change it to Rosetti."

The girl was trying to smile. She said, "A rose by any other name . . ."

Carmine laughed. Reina and Scarbo laughed. The babe just looked at her hands. After a moment, Carmine asked her, "What do you do, Miss Rosetti?"

"Did you say what or how?"

"I said what. For a living."

"I don't think that's any of your business, is it?"

"I'm making it. What do you do?"

She showed him her teeth with what was probably supposed to be a smile. "Whatever I can," she replied. "Like you."

That one scored. Carmine laughed it up and took a pull at his coke. He was enjoying this broad. Scarbo and Reina were enjoying her, also—but they knew what was going down here and they were keeping their place.

Carmine asked her, "Where's your fella?"

"Frankie?" She shrugged, and tried another smile.

Carmine's voice took a hard turn. "No damn games, honey. Where is he?"

"He left just behind you," she replied, the voice shaking again now. "I don't know where he went. He asked me to take the call if it came. It came and I took it. So shoot me. What's all the mystery? What's going on?"

"I've been waiting for you to tell me what's going on," Carmine told her, the voice getting dangerously soft.

"I don't know what's going on," the broad came right back at him. "And I don't know anything about Frankie. I wish I'd never seen him. Or *you!* Now are you going to let me—"

"Shut up!"

She did.

"Fuzz?"

"Yessir."

"What's in her purse?"

"Just the usual junk."

"How much money?"

"A hundred bucks, even. In shiny new twenties."

"Where'd you get the hundred, honey? Frankie lay it on you?"

"Go to hell!"

"Show her, Fuzz."

Martin stepped forward and slapped the broad from behind. It sounded like a pistol shot and it turned her head, nearly spilling her out of the chair. Tears were starting down the shiny cheeks and the voice was shaking but

125

mad as hell as she told Carmine, "Don't go crazy! This is all . . . insane! If it's that important, I'll tell you! What do you want?"

"I want your boyfriend."

"Wonderful! When you find him, have your big thug here give him one for me, will you! I didn't know he was a . . . a . . ."

"A *what*?"

"A gangster," she replied quietly.

Carmine chuckled. All the bosses were smiling. The guys upstairs had been drawn by the pistol-shot slap and were watching with interest.

"What makes you think he's a gangster?" Carmine asked her.

"Look . . . he wanted me to go to Louisville with him. That's all. It was a fun thing. Next I know we're in Indiana. I don't know what . . . what . . ."

Venturi edged around to get a better look at the broad. A chill was creeping along his spine and it must have reached his face because Carmine had suddenly decided to acknowledge his presence.

"Something bothering you, Harry?"

"Yessir. I was just wondering . . . who is this guy Frankie? What's he look like?"

"You don't know?"

"I'm not sure. That's why—"

"He knows *you*, Harry. Said all your boys are dead. Said you sent him over here to find me."

The words escaped Venturi's lips before he

126

knew he was going to utter them. "Jesus *Christ*!"

The broad was giving him a very, very scared look.

And Carmine wasn't looking so hot himself, of a sudden, from deep beneath that genial mask. "Who is the guy, Harry?" he asked through wooden lips.

"Bolan," Venturi croaked. "I guess it's Mack Bolan. He laid all over us at Stoney Lonesome."

None of the bosses were smiling now. And the broad started crying again.

Carmine was on his feet. "You're just now giving me this?" he snarled. "We find you holed up in Columbus and you're just now giving me *this*?"

Venturi knew that he'd blown it clear out the window, but he was still trying. "It's not like that, Carmine—please! I thought I'd led the guy off! I didn't tell 'im about this joint. I didn't even *know* about this joint! Alla my boys were dead. All but *me*! See? I figure he's setting me up. He wants me to spring and run to *you*. I ran the other way, Carmine! And I was afraid to call or anything. We all know how that guy is—he gets onto everything! I didn't even want to *call*! Hell—I didn't *know* where to call. I was just—"

"You were just laying in a hole and shivering!" Carmine yelled. "Why didn't you tell Fuzz or Willie about it when they found you?"

"Because I figured I lost him! I *knew* I lost him. And I figured—I didn't want to cause a

127

panic. I wanted to report to you, straight and quiet."

"You been here five minutes now, Harry!"

"Yessir and I just been waiting my chance. I *told* you. Didn't I tell you? Just now?"

By now, yeah, he'd told the whole joint.

Gulacci was coming back up the hill, about six of his boys suddenly swarming around him in a protective envelope.

Scarbo and Reina were on their feet and pacing nervously, casting anxious glances here and there.

All the second-echelon guys from the porch upstairs were hurrying down to join the nervous circle at the patio level.

And Carmine Tuscanotte was just fit to be tied.

Venturi could see it all, now—the whole rap. Carmine had invited all the bosses down to Brown County for a quiet parley in the trees—a "now or never" parley, which could only mean the reformation of the Outfit. With a bunch as nervous and edgy as this one, Carmine must have really laid on a heavy security sell. He'd gone to all this trouble and expense to make the other bosses feel safe and secure.

And now this.

Venturi could understand and sympathize with his boss's rage.

It had all come down to this.

Mack the Bastard was probably somewhere out in those woods right now—preparing hell-fire. Or he could even be walking among them, taking their pulse and waiting his chance.

But there was one sweet note to it all. Harry the Apeman was still the best cock on the roost. Any thought of disciplinary action would have to await another time. Carmine instinctively turned to the cock he trusted the most.

"Get it hard, Harry!" he snarled. "I want a line of steel all around this damn place!"

And Harry would see to that, sure. But he'd stood eyeball to eyeball with Mack the Bastard—had felt the guy's ice and tasted his heat. It would take more than a ring of steel to stop that guy.

He turned a commanding gaze to Fuzz Martin. "Stay with the broad," he ordered. "Sweat her, but keep her whole. If Frankie is Bolan then that's our ace. I want to know what he's got and what he's after."

Martin turned questioning eyes to the boss.

Carmine nodded and said, "He's the cock, Fuzz. Do what he says."

Damn right he was the the cock.

And he would stop at nothing to carve Mack the Bastard down to size. And then he'd step on that fuckin' *cockroach* and spread his guts all over Brown County.

But the woman was the key. He was sure of that. Which was why he'd given her to Fuzznuts. The guy would enjoy every ounce of sweat she dropped.

But Mack Bolan would not. Hell no—Mack Bolan would not.

CHAPTER 13

A TIME FOR WAR

Bolan had called off the scouting expedition the moment he spotted April Rose. Nor did he consider it too great a loss. He'd already confirmed the defensive set at the joint and eyeballed enough of the denizens to verify the major nameplates. Scarbo was there, and Reina—for sure. Also he'd made a couple of guys who were thought to be closely associated with Gumball Gulacci, a guy who'd made a humble start in the rackets with punchboards and gumball machines, then parlayed that small venture into total domination of vending machines in several Illinois counties.

At last tally, Gulacci owned a number of key politicians and was regarding most of Southern Illinois as his own inviolable turf. He was now thought to be a likely candidate alongside

Tuscanotte for eventual ownership of the midwestern U.S.

So Bolan had his set. There were no doubts about what was there and what was going down. It was no casual gathering of thieves. It was little Miami, sure—and no doubt a king of knaves would emerge from that conclave.

As for the defenses—all of that was in the basket now, anyway. The reappearance of Harry Venturi made that a certainty. A Bolan alarm would go down, for sure, and the defensive set would move into a panic hard. So much for that. Bolan should have cooked that guy— and probably he would have, white flag or no, had he known at the time that such a major showdown was looming.

All that was past and deserving of no further thought. Venturi was here, the die was cast, and April Rose, the lover, was caught in the middle. That was the all of it. Those people up there would have no difficulty divining her place in all this. And they would have no compunction whatever about using her in any manner that would serve their needs.

So time was of the double essence, now. Whatever could be done must be done—as quickly and as vigorously as possible. That, Bolan knew, was the only prayer for April Rose.

He was off the bluff and moving quickly into the pines within seconds after that vehicle with its precious cargo crossed the dam. He had noted, earlier, the tire tracks in the clay, which told the route of the roving trailbike patrol— and he could hear, now, the whine of the small engine as it labored up the incline from the grasslands. In about thirty seconds, the guy should be approaching the crest of the hill at the northeast corner—and Bolan desired to be there ahead of him.

He was.

A narrow roadway had been carved along the ridge to run just above the east side of the lake. It was hardly more than a jeep trail, and it plunged down that east ridge from above the north end of the lake and crossed over at lake level to the west ridge, running along another but much smaller dam before climbing abruptly into the high country on the other side. A catch basin, or something, occupied swampy and impassable ground to the immediate north of there.

The motorcycle trail, though, traversed the far east boundary of the property along the ridgeline, moving in through the pine groves to the crest at the northeast corner before taking the dramatic drop to the lake. And those groves had not been planned for mature trees.

The little vehicle came up over the hill in existent and—except for the narrow truck-access trails that occurred at about every fifth row—there was not even walking room between the trees. Even the trucking trails had been encroached upon by the lateral extension of the growing pines. There was barely clearance for a motorcycle—and, even so, a guy would run the risk of a small limb in the face, now and then.

It was probably this consideration that dictated the path of the motorcycle patrol. There was evidence that the guy had yanked off small face-slappers along the way to insure himself a clear trail.

So much for comfort.

It was here that Bolan intended to snare himself a rider.

He noosed one end of a garrote onto the feathered end of an extending limb and stretched it taut to another limb on the other side of the trail, then took cover in the overlapping growth as the cyclist approached.

The little vehicle came up over the hill in low gear, the handlebars grazing outstretched branches on either side—and the guy was shifting up and winding her out when he hit the nylon barrier. He saw it an instant too late and was trying to dodge beneath when it caught him square in the mouth.

The tethered limbs gave a little—perhaps ten inches—then snapped taut and straightened the guy out in midair and slammed him to the ground on his back. The little bike traveled on unattended for another ten feet or so before plowing into the trees.

The unseated cyclist was bleeding at the mouth and wheezing for lost breath, which was never to be regained. A combat boot saw to that, unemotionally applied to the throat and crushing the larynx.

Bolan left the guy where he lay and went to retrieve the motorcycle. It was a Yamaha trailbike with an 80cc engine. A ten-year-old kid could of handled it. Standard rockerbar gear shift, handlebar clutch and accelerator, kick starter. The lay-down had not hurt it a bit.

He stashed the Weatherby and swung aboard, fired her up, and took her back down the hill.

Once clear of the pines, the trail dipped momentarily into the marshlands, then came into green lawn alongside the creek. He could see the bridge fifty yards ahead and the two sentries still chucking the football back and forth. They paid no attention to the noisy approach of the bike until Bolan was within spitting distance. The guy closest to him looked up, then, and did a doubletake before spiking the football and trying to do-or-die dive toward safety.

But Bolan's long legs had already lifted him clear and the little bike was spurting forward unmanned. It plowed into the diving man at high speed, then man and machine tumbled to the ground in a rolling wrestling match in which the machine was clearly dominant.

The other guy was in a whirling break for gunleather . . . a shade too late. The Beretta had leapt into Bolan's ready hand the instant the handlebar left it, and was chugging silent flame at the dancing sentry. The guy completed the whirl on his nose, and stayed there.

The first one was groaning beneath the weight of the Yamaha and bleeding from several exits. He was pretty badly busted up. The Beretta sent a quiet mercy round between clenched teeth to complete the job and retire the side.

Bolan did not recognize either of these guys. They were probably "stakers"—raw meat hired from the city cesspools to do or die for dimes and dollars. That they had died for their dollars was of no particular moral concern for Mack Bolan. A man who sells his soul cannot beggar the collector.

He removed a belt-clip key ring from one and dumped both bodies into the creek below the bridge, then unlocked the chainblock and threw the whole thing in.

Then he took the motorcycle up the back way to the small house on the east bank. He was reading this one as the guardshack—though it was certainly no shack in the literal sense, but a very stylish and obviously new studio-type chalet with a thirty-foot-high wall of glass in front and wraparound sundeck.

Bolan parked the Yamaha in the carport and entered through the rear. It had a large living room with a stone fireplace serving as a divider from a narrow Pullman-style kitchen which ran along the back wall. A small dining area opened along the west wall from the kitchen, elling into the living room. Two guys in their scivvies sat in there, playing a subdued game of cards. They neither saw nor heard what had come for them. Perhaps neither knew that he died with a Parabellum hollow-nose in the ear.

The glass-fronted living room looked over the sundeck and onto the grassy front grounds far below. Anyone standing where Bolan was now standing could have witnessed the attack on the bridge. Apparently none had been standing there.

Along a short hallway toward the east were bedrooms and a bath. Some guy was singing in the shower. Bolan went in there and pulled back the shower curtain. The guy stopped singing damn quick and made a grab for the Beretta. Bolan allowed him one small chunk from there and went on to check out the bedrooms. All were empty, now, but bore evidence of casual usage.

These had been the station keepers. Seven of them. And seven were down.

The hardsite east of the lake was now a comfort zone for Mack Bolan. For the moment, anyway—and there were damn few of those to spare.

April Rose would, no doubt, attest to that.

Bolan went back to the Yamaha and made fast tracks toward Clay Lick Road and his battle cruiser.

He meant to seal that joint.

One thing the boys had apparently not considered in their search for comfort: a sanctuary could very easily and very quickly become a mausoleum—even a two-zillion acre sanctuary . . . with the only exit sealed.

"Hang on, April," he sent word into the universal matrix where thoughts are things. *"Help is coming!"*

CHAPTER 14

POSITIONS

This was what he had meant. And she felt betrayed. Not by him but by the cutesy world of rose-colored glasses, which had raised her in naivete and educated her with pedantic nonsense.

Yes, this was what he'd meant—what he'd tried to warn her against—this savage world of brutal men within whom not the faintest flicker of humanity stirred.

Worse than anything else—stronger, even, than the clawing fear that was now shrinking her insides—was the jolting realization of her own stupidity and ignorance, the memory of her holier-than-thou putdown of that good man. She had actually presumed to lecture *him* about the nobility of the world—and all the while she'd been sitting in the shadow of a noble giant, baiting him with cute phrases learned from social theorists and pedantic midgets while he struggled to give her a crash course in the survival arts.

A good soldier uses every tool available.

The object is to get the job done and come out alive.

It's warfare, lady, and all the rules of war apply.

There are fiends afoot. . . . True, so true. And this one was now locking her into a dank, windowless basement storeroom and preparing to sweat her for cooperation.

But sweat was hardly the word.

She was saying, "This really isn't necessary, you know. We can—" when he stunned her with another of those hammy blows to the side of the head and sent her rolling across the concrete floor.

"Get up!" he growled.

She felt utterly ridiculous. Her knees were skinned and burning and she'd turned a finger back. She had momentary double vision and the room was tilted all askew.

. . . and come out alive. . .

She told the big goon, "This is crazy!"

"Get up!"

"I can save you a lot of trouble."

"No trouble at all, honey." He bent over her and lifted her by the front of the dress, setting her on her feet like a baby. Then he ripped the whole dress away with one savage pull.

She cried, "Now wait a minute!"

He was not waiting for anything, though. The bra came away with another brutal wrench and she knew pain such as she had never imagined as he swung her around by both breasts and flung her against the wall.

"In the name of *God*!" she wailed.

But he was bending over her again, leering down at her, clammy hands at the waistband of her panties. A big fist sank painfully into her tummy as he tore those away, also. Her ID slithered off onto the floor. He grabbed it, took one quick look, and said, "Well I'll be damned."

. . . uses every tool available.

"That's what I've been trying to tell you," she moaned. "You want the same thing I want. And you're screwing up my assignment."

"This means nothing to me," he growled.

"I'd really like to talk to your boss. It's very important!"

He chuckled wickedly. "Important to *you*, huh?"

"Important to *him*!" she cried.

It was obvious that the big goon was unhappy with this development. He *wanted* to hurt her. He was getting *kicks*. But he palmed the wallet and told her, "We'll see. Don't go away, huh? We got a lot of fun ahead."

"Thanks, I'll pass," she said. Or maybe she only thought it. The room was swimming around her.

He went out and locked the door behind him.

She lay there for a moment trying to clear her head. She felt sick at the stomach and pain was shrieking in from various parts of the body. But she also felt . . . what? Humiliated? Violated? Mad as hell, for sure. This was what

139

it was like to be raped. The anger, the frustration, the . . . *indignity*!

She managed to get onto her knees—and that felt even worse. Stark naked, soiled all over, utterly helpless . . . mad as hell!

No. April Rose did not love all mankind.

There are corruptions in the translation from force to form.

All you're listening with is your mind. And it's not stretched far enough to hear.

So okay, noble giant. Just be patient. April's mind was becoming more elastic by the moment.

But how many moments were left?

Venturi was presiding over a crash meeting of crew chiefs, trying to weld an effective fighting force from the diverse elements present. As head cock of the host delegation, this was his prerogative. Indeed, it was his responsibility.

The bosses themselves were clumped at the big stone fireplace—and apparently there was some problem with Gulacci. Which was dumb. All the problem should be *out there*—not *in here*.

Each moment that passed was vital, and they had to get the defenses set, with no more of this dicking around between the bosses. But their position was very strong, really. There was no need for panic. That was the idea that Venturi was trying to present to the crew chiefs—and he was speaking loudly enough for the bosses to hear it, also.

But then Fuzz Martin came bustling up. Hell, he hadn't been gone a minute! Prob'ly *killed* the broad, the dumb . . .

But, no. It was something else. The ex-cop's eyes were glazed some and he was breathing just a bit hard as he handed over a thin, card-sized wallet.

"Dumb broad!" he sneered. "Had it in her panties." He snickered and winked at a crew crief. "Wouldn't that be the last place to hide something important?"

Carmine stepped over from the fireplace to inquire, "What is it, Harry?"

Venturi passed the little wallet on to his boss as he unemotionally reported, "She's a federal cop."

"That doesn't figure," Tuscanotte said quietly, staring at the ID. The disturbed gaze shifted to Fuzz Martin. "What does she say?"

"Says she has something important to tell you."

"So why didn't she?"

Martin shrugged. "Says we blew her case."

"Meaning what?"

"Meaning, I guess, Bolan."

Carmine took that under advisement, rolling it through his brain a couple of times for fit. Then he asked, "How do you feel about it, Fuzz? You're the police expert."

"Could be, yeah," the ex-cop replied. "I guess they want the guy as much as we do."

"But I mean how does it *feel* to you?"

"I feel like she's not hurting enough yet, Carmine. This was just the first pop. She

141

hasn't started busting and bawling yet. Right now she's just yodeling."

Tuscanotte frowned.

Venturi added his thoughts to it. "None of that really matters, Carmine. The *matter* is that she's Bolan's woman. Forget the undercover. If he doesn't *know*—and how could he if she's still in the picture? Listen, broads are the guy's weak point. He's nearly blown himself two or three times over a broad. Hell, it all *started* over a broad. Didn't it?"

"So I hear," Tuscanotte mused. He pulled at his nose and said, "The Achilles heel, eh?"

"That's exactly it. An undercover cop won't help us a damn bit, right now. And there's always the problem of afterwards. How much did she see? How much did she hear? What does she know that will come back to haunt us later? That broad is a *tool*, Carmine—not an ally."

"Maybe you're right."

"I'm going to play it that way."

"Okay, play it. It's your department."

Venturi sighed with relief and said, "Yessir." He turned to Fuzz Martin. "Keep the sweat on. But listen, Fuzz, dammit—you leave her in one piece, able to talk and able to walk. I mean it. When the time comes, I want that broad whole."

Willy Frio danced in at that moment, very agitated, and busted into the parley. "The road's blocked," he announced, very unhappily. "How the hell can I get a force down the hill with the damn road blocked? This is—Mr. Gulacci's boys are making a convoy out there. I can't get a damn thing through."

Gulacci called over from the fireplace, "Relax, Willy. We'll be out of your way in a minute."

"What's he mean by that?" Venturi growled loudly.

"Gummo is bailing out," Tuscanotte said, sotto voce. "He doesn't like our little retreat."

"That's crazy!" Venturi yelled. "Pardon me, Mr. Gulacci, but it's crazy and I have to say it! We could hold off a marine force up here! But you'll be so much raw meat down there on that road! I can't be responsible!"

"Nobody's asking," Gulacci said quietly. "We got ourselves here, we'll get ourselves out. But I'm telling you *you're* crazy if you think you can sit here and hold against that Bolan guy. I seen what he did to *Don* Gio, and I seen what he did at Miami, and I'm tellin' you the guy comes on like panzers. It ain't just guns, Harry. It's bombs and rockets and the goddam kitchen sink. And I for one am not stayin' around and waitin' for that. I say we should all go out, together. Call ahead, if we got to, and ask for police escort. I'm not proud. I'd love to see a convoy of black and whites come rolling up here right now, I tell you. Let the little lady blow her whistle and bring the goddam feds in here, I don't care. Better that than what you're waiting for. Listen. I saw it all the minute I seen this joint. This is what the guy loves—all of us mobbed up and stuck away some place in the sticks so he can just—"

143

"We got a *hundred boys* here, Mr. Gulacci!"

"Say, you stick those hundred boys right up your ass, Harry. No offense, Carmine. But I have to say it like I see it. If you got a broad here that the guy wants, I say send her to him. Strike a deal. That's my advice to you. For me, I'm cutting out."

"I'll have the guy's head in my pocket, Gummo," Tuscanotte woodenly declared. "I'll run it through the streets of Chicago on a pole, then I'll run it through the streets of New York. I'll run it to Detroit and Cleveland, L.A. and Dallas, and I'll run it up the damn flagpole at the U.N. And everybody will say that Carmine stood and took while Gummo crapped and slunk. If that's what you want, then go. We've been runnng enough from this guy. One guy. All the old men crapped and slunk while this one guy took us apart piece by piece. We've seen our thing fall apart and melt all around us. All the bluesuits and all the feds and all the armies of the world couldn't do it to us—but we crapped and slunk and let one damn guy do it to us. It's time to get our legs under us. It's time to be men. But you go ahead, Gummo. You crap and slink if that's what you want to do."

It was a hell of a speech. Venturi felt as though there should be applause after a speech like that. Carmine was getting legs, for damn sure. Harry the Apeman had picked himself a winner this time, for damn sure. The guy was taking a page from the books of Maranzano and Luciano. He was going to be the boss of bosses, by God. And Harry Venturi was, by God, going to be there with him.

There was plenty of applause, sure, but it was all in the eyes of those men assembled there at that fated moment.

Except for Gummo Gulacci.

Carmine must have wanted the greaseball to leave. Who would stay, after a spitbath like that one?

Gulacci went out of there in a hurry, leaving the door open behind him for anyone who might decide to follow.

None followed.

Fuzz Martin was the one to break the silence. "So what do I do with the broad?" he asked nobody in particular.

"Save her," Carmine said, very quietly.

"Whole," Venturi added. He watched the sadistic bastard walk away, then he turned to Willy Frio. "Soon as the gumball clears, move your boys down. I want them all on the east side. Take those two jerks off the gate and put your two best boys down there, with choppers. They stay covered and they shoot anything that shows on that bridge. Okay? Okay. Then I want a man every fifty feet along the creek. Every third man gets a boomer—and I want at least one chopper on the backup line for every five men staked along the creek. Got that?"

Frio nodded in understanding, but his eyes were showing a worry.

"Whatever you got left after that, I want them up on that ridge in the woods. I leave it to you how best to put them down. But you leave two boys for walking patrol, and I mean you keep them walking and checking every position you got over there. Anybody turns up missing, or you got any other suspicions at all, I want five quick shots in the air. You got it?"

"I got it," Frio replied. "But what's that going to do to you up here Harry? With Gummo gone, we only got about—"

"I know what we got, Willy. Anybody here cant's live with those odds had better maybe slink away with Gulacci."

"You call it, Harry," Scarbo called over. "My boys are standing."

"Mine, too," seconded Reina.

That was plenty good enough for Harry Venturi.

He went to the screen porch to watch the Gulacci convoy ease down the hill. Small loss. Twenty guns, at the most—and most of those gumball merchants, probably.

Gulacci's pure white Cadillac was second in line in the four-car caravan. It broke the corner of the house as the point vehicle nosed onto the dam and began the cautious progress to the other side.

Then something very remarkable came winging in over the lake—something fast, rustling through that calm sky with flame and smoke trailing out behind it.

It came so fast that Venturi had no time to react or even to wonder before it zipped into that point car, and lifted it into the air on a ball of fire, and blew it back up the hill in tumbling pieces of flaming junk.

The heat from that blast warmed Harry's face and the shock wave flung him back against the glass wall.

And as he was trying to pick himself up and collect his stunned mind, dazed eyes caught the trail of another whistler in the air an instant before it slammed into the pure white Cadillac.

Grand speeches and strutting legs had no meaning here.

Poor Gummo had maybe been right.

They had the guy exactly where he wanted them.

CHAPTER 15

STANDING HARD

Bolan had brought his cruiser back along Clay Lick Road and over the bridge to invade Divine Light in frontal assault. The approach remained clear and he encountered no obstacle as he powered along the lower drive. The road branched off at the base of the east ridge, one leg curving around toward the sentry house while the other climbed straight toward the earthen dam. Both came together again at the approach to the dam, the one being merely an elliptical offshoot from the main drive.

Bolan opted for the ellipse, circling around the house and plunging off onto the grassland behind it. The cruiser's front-wheel drive and airbag suspension was suited very well to off-road travel, so long as the terrain was not too rough. This was definitely marginal terrain and the going was rough, indeed, but he gained the crest of the hill with little difficulty and pulled his war machine into light cover at the edge of the pine grove. From here, he had excellent command of the entire west ridge, the lake from tip to tip, and most of the east ridge.

The two west bank houses were directly across the lake at a slight angle from his position—and at roughly the same elevation. And though the trees partially obstructed the view, there were intimations of a circular drive coming up from the dam and serving both houses atop that ridge. Vehicles were massed over there and quite a few were parked to the north of the A-frame, suggesting that perhaps the circle was not the only drive serving that side of the lake. He punched in the optics and undertook a close study of that latter consideration—striking paydirt almost instantly.

The natural contour of the land had formed a small lagoon with virtually perpendicular banks immediately north of the A-frame structure. And the close inspection revealed that it was not all natural contour over there; it was not a single, uninterrupted ridge that formed that west side. There was, instead, a separate finger extending on southerly beyond the ridge that formed most of the west bank of the lake.

Another, smaller, earthen dam rose up beyond that lagoon to bridge the fingers and provide terrain continuity—*and there was a skinny waterfall plunging from that level into the lagoon a hundred feet or so below.*

Closer probing located the source of the

waterfall—a section of pipe extending out from near the top of that small dam. It was an overflow device. There was another man-made lake up there, feeding its overflow into the lower lake.

Well damn! Bolan was wishing, now, that he'd had more time for a thorough recon.

The optics picked up a couple of guys walking across that high dam. Each carried a shotgun and wore sideleather. God only knew what else was up there.

But there was no time, now, to massage that question.

There was vehicular movement behind the main house—fragmented glimpses of a line of cars in motion.

The enemy was on the move.

Bolan energized the fire, bringing the roof pod to *raise and lock*. Then he scanned across the lakefront and locked the optics onto that hillside above the main dam as he punched in *fire enable*.

Glowing red rangemarks became superimposed upon the electronic grid of the optics, monitor as that line of cars eased down off the hill—four of them, in road caravan formation. That would put heavy guns at the point—a divine body enveloped somewhere in the middle within either the second or third vehicle and surrounded by living shields—another overweight gun crew or two bringing up the rear.

Bolan added infrared augmentation to the optic probe, searching interiors for a familiar face and finding it in the second vehicle—a big white Cadillac limousine with jumpseats in the rear and a gumball merchant huddled within that shield of flesh.

April was not there.

Too bad, for them.

He set up *target acquisition* for an automatic one-two, giving the point vehicle first honors and cycling on to the white bodyboat for the *auto-follow*—then he banged his knee and sent the first one streaking toward hot intercept at dam level.

The little bird rustled away in the target trajectory, found her path just above the treetops, then dipped in fiery closure.

She punched in just below the radiator grill and loosed her fire beneath the point vehicle, lifting it in spreading pieces and blowing those onto the following cars. The pieces were still settling when Firebird Two lifted away and went seeking a white Cadillac that was already in grave difficulty, skewered across the narrow drive and searching for comfort in a firestorm.

This one was programmed for doorpost elevation and she found her mark with a shattering impact that sheared off the roof and everything else protruding above the seat level, engulfing headless corpses in the fireball and pitching the entire flaming wreck over the side in a tumbling plunge down the face of the dam.

Two birds remained in the nest—but they were not needed in that disaster zone. The third member of the caravan was afire and the fourth had lost its grip on the hillside and was

151

sliding out of control into the steep canyon to the south.

There would be no further vehicular traffic across there—not without extensive repairs to the roadbed. The first strike had dug a sizeable crater and erased the road, leaving a four to six foot gap at the west end of the earthen dam.

A lot of foot traffic, though, was erupting behind the house and people were spilling out along the grassy slope of the front lawn, as well, seeking cover behind the occasional tree and shrub dotting that landscape. There was also a bit of activity over beyond the A-frame, with people scampering cautiously along the hillside above the lagoon.

So okay.

Monday's battle was underway.

And the only regrets of the moment were that he did not know the precise whereabouts of April Rose—and he did not know what lay upon that chaotic land beyond the smaller dam at the upper level.

One thing for sure, though—whatever plans or fiendish intentions they'd held for the lady would be definitely sidetracked for the moment. He'd provided her with some breathing room.

Now, dammit, if only he could make some *living* room for the pretty lady . . . and keep her pretty.

He fought away the mutilated visions of other once-pretty ladies of his past acquaintance—the little *soldata* of Miami who'd left him living poetry; the cute kid from

Manhattan who'd nursed his bleeding flesh, then left her own shreds on the cutting table of a weiner factory; the Ranger girl from Montreal who'd found her hellish truth in a ghoul chamber in Detroit and bequeathed a lifetime of waking nightmares for her rescuer ..., damn, *damn*!

Better death than that, April. Better quick and clean than ...

He wrenched it all away and concentrated on a scan of the big house. It was layered—stone and glass at the lower level, wood and glass plus a lot of wire screen upstairs. Two doors downstairs . . . one massive double of glass at the north end, another smaller wooden one with a single glass panel to the south. The double doors north opened onto a patio, now deserted. He punched up the infrared to laser-point brilliance for a probe beyond the facade and also brought up the barrel mikes for audio monitoring. Even without the directional pickups, sound-travel across the water was excellent, with voices carrying clear and sharp when uplifted in shouts and commands to the scurrying troops. Directionalized and amplified by the barrel pickups, even ordinary conversations could be monitored with relative ease.

There was a lot of confusion over there. Someone was yelling and armwaving a rescue operation for the survivors of the rocket stroke. Other guys were dashing about in frantic defensive preparations.

Bolan caught a ghostly red image of Paul Reina in the optic monitor, a fleeting frame of anxiety appearing momentarily behind the thick windowglass upstairs before quickly receding into the interior.

There was a lot of scrambling over there, yeah, in the immediate wake of the opening strike—and obviously they had not yet spotted the precise source of that strike.

Plenty soon enough they would.

He returned the visual scan to the lower level just in time to frame a most interesting figure emerging from the doubledoors onto the patio.

A ghoulish figure, yeah.

It was Fuzz Martin, crazycop, caught in a moment of indecision—the ugly face contorted in a play of conflicting emotions. Then he moved off across the patio toward the south end.

Toward that door down there, yeah.

Bolan had to wonder about that . . . but not for long. He had the door framed in fullscreen perspective and with full augmentation as the gun unlocked it, flung it open, and stepped inside.

And there was only a quick millisecond glimpse into that interior—but there *she* was, yeah—the ladylove, stripped naked and crouching just inside, a three-foot iron pipe or some similar weapon thrust forward defiantly in a fencing stance. It was a snap glimpse, glowing with the unreal, hellish hues of infrared.

Then that door swung closed, leaving an even more hellish picture in Bolan's mind.

His heart had leapt over there to join that gutsy lady. She'd found herself some *hard*—and she'd found a weapon, to whatever pointless effect—and by God she was not going down whimpering.

She was standing to it.

But Bolan could find more than *heart* to send her. There were still two birds in the nest, and the rangemarks leapt to the command as he swung that scan toward vital meat.

He could send her more than heart, yeah.

He could send her some *doubledamnhard*.

CHAPTER 16

PLAYING IT

This was awful, it was terrible. The whole damn front of the house was made of glass and—it was terrible—there was no place to . . .

He grabbed Carmine by the arm and urgently whispered, "This's no good! That guy is throwing heavy artillery at us! He could just as easy brought the joint down around our ears!"

"Then why didn't he?" Tuscanotte growled shakily. "Why's he playing with us?"

"You better believe he's got his reasons. He must know the broad is here. If he don't see her pretty soon . . ."

"Do what you think you gotta do, Harry! You're the cock. Just do it!"

Venturi was still whispering. "Right now I'm worried about—you know this joint better than I do—ain't there some place you can harden out for a little while? You'n the other bosses?"

"Downstairs in the back, yeah—the furnace room. It's right under the kitchen. The walls are cement block and stone. You suggest it."

The head cock should suggest it, sure. They were all scared out of their skulls, these bosses. Nobody had more to lose than they did—and they were the most scared of all. But they wouldn't want to show it, no.

Venturi raised his voice in the urgent "suggestion."

"Mr. Tuscanotte, I think you should take Mr. Scarbo and Mr. Reina down to the hard room. Just for sure—okay? I don't like all this glass up here. We don't want to make it any easier for the guy than we have to. Right?"

"You're right, Harry," Tuscanotte replied with a loud sigh. He chuckled as he turned to the others. "Paul? Natty? Let's give the boys a break, eh."

They were damned glad to give the boys a break, sure. Tuscanotte led them down the inside stairway, making a big joke of the quick retreat.

So much for that. So now what the hell?

It was quiet, for the moment. The guy had hit them twice then laid back. For why? Well . . . look at the hits. A line of cars coming down off the hill. Why that? Why not the houses?

Sealed!

That was it! The bastard sealed the hill!

Why?

157

Was he planning on coming over—on foot?—to walk among them and slit throats and blast eyeballs?

Naw. *Naw*! That was no percentage play! Look at what he'd done by just laying back and sending two blasts from far away! Wiped out a whole damn convoy, f'Christ's sake! Knocked off a big boss! Put the whole damn place in panic and covering assholes!

It was the broad. Sure it was. So . . . how to play her? Did they hold her for a shield or send her over as a plea bargain? That damn crazy Fuzz was . . .

Venturi turned to a crew captain and snarled. "Where's Fuzz?"

"He was here a minute ago," the guy replied. "He came running in here right after Gummo got it. But I guess he . . ."

"Run down and see! I want the broad up here, right now! Don't let Fuzz tell you no different! You get me?"

The crew captain got him. He touched his hardware and ran down the stairs.

At that precise instant, another whistler came across. Venturi instinctively threw himself toward the back wall; it looked for all the world as though that thing was headed straight for him. And maybe it had been. It plowed in down below somewhere, lifting the floor in a puff beneath him and sending those glass walls to popping and quivering in their frames. Somebody down there screamed like in a nightmare and came running up the stairs enveloped in flames.

It was the crew captain—*poor bastard!*—ablaze from head to foot.

Venturi scrambled clear and pumped three quick shots into the human torch, ending that torment—but the corpse blazed on, melting into the deep carpet and starting a fire in the upholstery of a large couch.

Venturi danced away and ran outside to the rear. The whole northeast corner of the joint was on fire, flames licking up from the lower level and engulfing the screened porch.

And that wasn't all of it. Another whizzer zipped across Venturi's frenzied gaze and plowed into the A-frame, torching the structure instantly and scattering blazing boards and roofing along the hillside behind it.

Willie Frio yelled, "Jesus, Harry! What do we do?"

"Take cover!" Venturi yelled back.

"I got these two guys from Indianapolis! What do I do with them?"

"Give 'em a fuckin' plane ticket!" Venturi snarled savagely. The least of his goddam worries were the goddam fuckin' corruptions from the capital! In his corner vision he'd glimpsed a boy tumbling down the hill behind the A-frame, now another—*those were dead men's falls!*—then even a third before the deep thunder of a heavy rifle in rapid fire began rolling across those hills.

Shit! The guy was taking everything he could get! And he was getting plenty!

Someone down on the front lawn yelled, "*I see 'im!*"

159

"*I see nothing*!" screamed another.

"Watch the tops of those trees over there! *There*! See that?"

"I seen it, yeah."

What? Was the guy walking on treetops now?

Return fire was beginning to crackle across the front grounds, now. And Venturi prayed that those boys were not shooting at mere *hope*.

He skirted warily around the burning corner of the house and made a run for a tree at the far side of the patio. Just as he reached it, he saw two boys with choppers beginning a cautious, heads-down advance along the back side of the dam. Somebody was thinking, thank God. He hoped that others were, also—and, yeah, *knew* that they were. Some. These were not all nickle-and-dime poolhall punks with an itch for glory. Some were real professionals from the hard old days and knew what to do when hard times came.

That was okay, that was great. Venturi was head cock, though, and it was his job to see that those hard times never arrived. So he'd screwed up, and let them come. But all of that had not been his fault. Most of it was Carmine's doing, with his tippy-toe approach and insane secrecy. So now it was Venturi's job to see that the hard times went away, for good and all.

He kicked open the door to the storeroom and knew that he'd gotten there just in time. Fuzz had the broad stark naked and by the throat, alternately slapping her and kneeing her in the crotch. Her eyes were rolling and she was probably only about half conscious. Blood was flowing down Fuzz's face from a nasty crack above the eyes and he was plumb, grunting crazy.

Venturi popped him across the back of the head with the pistol butt—and had to do it twice to get the crazy bastard's attention.

"I told you to leave her *whole*!" Venturi yelled. "You outta your goddam mind? The joint's burning down around you and you're in here assin' your kicks?"

"She's got it coming," Martin panted, eyeing him crazily. He wiped the blood from his brows and said, "Came at me with a steel stake. I'm going to shove it up her snatch to the *hilt*!"

Venturi knew that the guy meant it. And he still meant to do it.

"The hell you are," he told him, and pumped two shots into that ugly face. He never liked the crazy bastard, anyway. Carmine loved him, sure. So let Carmine bury him. He picked up the girl and carried her out of there.

"Are you okay, little lady?" he asked her.

She was having too much trouble with her breathing to reply coherently—but he could see that she was going to be all right. God she was beautiful, even in this shape. Fuzz Martin's blood was smeared all over her—and maybe even a little bit of her own—but there was nothing here that would not soon heal and be quickly forgotten.

But, now, what the hell did he do with her?

How to play it? Did Bolan really *want* her? If so, how badly?

He staggered down the hill with his burden, speaking softly to her and trying to soothe her the way he would his own kid. Maybe he had a kid like this . . . somewhere . . . maybe.

Halfway down the hill, he yelled at a popeyed group taking cover behind a stack of cut logs. "I want a shirt! A *white* shirt! One of you boys take off your goddam shirt!"

He knew how to play it.

Harry the Apeman knew exactly how to play it.

CHAPTER 17

THE PRAYER

He sent one into the far corner of the house, knowing full well that it woud blow fire and destruction into that joint, but taking a calculated risk that the havoc would not immediately spread to the side where April Rose was being tormented. And perhaps the hit would spread enough confusion and panic to provide a bit more breathing room for the lady.

But he had to keep the pressure on. The final bird he sent to the A-frame, going for the greatest effect. And he got it, instantly converting that whole joint into a flaming ruin.

Then he took the Weatherby up to the roof and began laying into them from above the treetops—seeking numbers only, not tactical effect, going for the easy hits in a pointed desire to spread only fear and confusion.

He was buying time.

And the price tag on that buy was pretty high.

They spotted his general position very quickly and he could see movements everywhere as the counteroffensive got underway. The return fire became very hot, very quick—forcing him to break off and quietly move the warwagon into new concealment—but that was not the real concern.

The real concern was that they would succeed in moving some troops across to his side—and then he would be in real trouble.

This was not Bolan's chosen combat posture. He much preferred to be the active aggressor—the quiet infiltrator—or the wily guerrilla visiting havoc with a quick hit and run. It was simply not smart tactics to attempt a longterm one-man siege against a clearly superior enemy encampment—no matter how great the firepower on that one man's side of the picture. With a determined enemy, superior numbers would ultimately prevail. He did not know how determined they may be. He did know their numbers, and there was no comfort in that knowledge.

He did not like this tactic, no.

But it was the one dealt him by the moment. He had no alternative but to work it for everything it could yield.

If only . . .

He tossed that thought out. There was no time or energy for iffing it. April *was* there and Bolan had to play it that way.

164

But then, from somewhere out of the matrix, came an echo of some words he'd offered to the lady—just a short few hours ago. It seemed a lifetime. This kind of life had a way of expanding time as well as shrinking it.

A good soldier will use every tool available.

He could not think of April Rose as a tool, of course. But the word fit, nonetheless. She was the tool of this present situation, around which everything else was draped.

She could be the tool of his total defeat.

But . . . wasn't it true that in every defeat there stood also the potential for victory? So often, wasn't it a mere breath or a heartbeat that meant the final difference between victory and defeat?

A good soldier will use . . .

Yeah. Okay. He'd told the lady something else, as well. He'd told her that it was not a game of good versus bad, but *warfare*—and that all the rules of warfare applied. He'd been trying to make her see that good did not always win—that very often it lost the war. Tell it to the Jews of the Holocaust, April, that the world is basically good and that *right* is *might*.

Nor did it work the other way. Might is not always right, of course—but, dammit, the greatest might always wins! Tell it to the doe being devoured by the wolf that God is Love. Tell it to the bird in the jaws of the cat—tell it to the cat in the jaws of the dog—tell it to the desperate man of the ghetto whose kids are cold and hungry—tell it . . .

Oh *God*! What did it all *mean*?

Okay. It meant, yeah, that Mack Bolan was a warrior. He'd looked back along that dark and fearful road and he'd seen the dreadful fiend treading softly behind. That fiend was stalking all mankind—and all the desperate prayers of a threatened world had not deterred it. Hell . . . it *thrived* on weakness and grew fat on futile prayers.

"God will not look you over for medals, diplomas, or degrees—but for *scars*!"[1]

The guy who said that had been there, and he'd known.

If there was a God in heaven then He had not built this turbulent world to *love* it, nor for *it* to love *Him*. He'd built a crucible, not a playground. He'd constructed a challenge, not an easement.

Bolan knew that *God* was *growth*. . .

And this was Mack Bolan's prayer. It was not a futile one, but directed straight into the heart of the matter.

Dear God, give me hard; and give me soft; and give me the heart to handle both.

Make me a good soldier, when the cause is right.

And when I am a dead soldier—look at my scars and say that I have been well built in that crucible called Earth, that I have been a worthy tool of the cosmic game.

He now added another, in deference to the

[1] *Elbert Hubbard, Amer. Writer and Publisher;* d.1915

166

pretty lady who'd found her hard in the jaws of the fiend.

Make me right, this time.
This time, let my heart be pure!

CHAPTER 18

THE DEAL

The kid had been waving the white shirt for most of a minute and growing more and more nervous about it when finally an electronically amplified voice came off that hill over there and filled the lake with those same quiet, assured tones that had come down at him from the stairway at Stoney Lonesome.

It was a bit unnerving, and the boys behind him on the hillside felt it, too. What kind of damn guy was this?—and what did he have up there? What kind of damned machinery had he brought with him?

"I see your flag, Harry. What's on your mind?" ..

"Can you hear me?" Venturi shouted at the top of his lungs.

"Much too well. Just keep looking this way

*and use a normal voice. I can hear you breath-
ing, guy."* ..

Well now *that* was unnerving as hell.

"Can you see this little lady I got here?"
Venturi asked in a quiet, conversational
voice—testing that.

"I can. What'd you do to her?"

Venturi sent a perplexed look to the troops
behind him, then turned back to that strange
conversation with the lake.

"She's okay, Mr. Bolan. I wanted you to see
that. She's okay."

*"I'd like to see her standing on her own,
Harry."* ..

Venturi whispered furiously at the girl,
"Think you can do it, honey? You *got* to do it!"

She was still a bit out of it and her reply
was breathless and fuzzy. "Where is he? Tell
him I'm all right."

But the guy heard even that. *"I'm very near,
April. Don't hang it up, yet. Put the shirt on
her, Harry. And send your boy back up the
hill."* ..

Venturi eased the girl to her feet, but
continued supporting her as he gestured angrily to the kid with the white flag. They
tucked her into the shirt and the kid got the
hell off that pier gladly. Venturi overheard him
saying to somebody, as he retreated up the hill,
"Hell, I dunno. He's just standin' there talkin'
like to the fishes and the guy's coming right
back at him every time."

Venturi fastened the most strategic buttons
in place and said to the fishes, "You're right, I

169

should've covered her. I wanted you to see that she's all here."

"I spot a couple of your boys on the dam, Harry. Do you send them back or do I?"

There was no need for either. Those boys immediately began sending themselves back. And Harry Venturi didn't blame them. This was spooky as hell.

He quietly told that disembodied voice out there, "I also want you to know, Mr. Bolan, that I did not spit on your white flag—over there, you know. They come and got me. It's important you know that. I didn't know about this joint, neither. I hope you believe it."

This was strange, very strange. Both joints burning behind him, dead bodies littering the whole place, forty or fifty more boys pressed to the earth with heads and asses down—and here stood the head cock on a pier in the lake with a nearly naked broad leaning against him, holding a quiet conversation as if with God Himself.

It was weird, yeah—and don't think those boys behind him weren't sharing that weirdness.

"I believe it, yeah. What's on your mind?"

"I know you keep your word, Mr. Bolan. I come down here to strike a deal. You've hurt us real bad. Mr. Gulacci is dead. Maybe half our boys are dead. I'm giving it to you level, see. If this keeps on, we'll prob'ly all end up dead. Even the little lady, here. I say it's dumb. I say nobody here wants anything that bad. If I got your word, I'll send you the lady. And we

170

call it even. That's all I wanted to say. That's my offer."

"It's an attractive offer. But it's not even. Not nearly even, Harry. You can offer more than that."

"What? What can I offer more than that? I'm saying take the broad and beat it. We got fifty boys to bury over here."

"I didn't come here for the broad. I didn't come here for fifty boys and a gumball boss. You know what I came for, Harry."

He couldn't believe it. That guy was . . . "You talking about Carmine?"

"And a couple more, yeah."

The nervy son of a bitch wanted all the bosses! "Hey, I couldn't—that's not reasonable!" He peered over his shoulder and up the hill. "Are you saying I should? . . ."

"I'm the only one can hear you, Harry. Talk like men. I'm not telling you what you have to do. I'm telling you what I have to do. If I have to walk over fifty more boys to do it, then okay. But I have to agree with you, it's kind of dumb. From their standpoint, anyway."

Somebody up the slope loudly inquired, "What's he talking about? What's he want?"

Venturi threw a snarling "Shut up!" back there. Those boys, of course, were hearing only one side of this conversation. Bolan's side. Which was okay. Yeah, that was okay.

"I can't send you the bosses, Mr. Bolan. Look, I already took out Fuzz Martin. He's the guy was roughing up this little lady. I took him out—and I have Carmine's blessing on that.

Listen—you already killed it for him here. I mean you blew his whole parley. They'll never listen to him again. If that's what's bothering you—I mean . . ."

"I'll make you a deal, Harry. Is the lady okay enough to paddle a canoe?"

The girl said raggedly, "Sure, and I could tow a battleship behind me. Just show me that canoe."

"Did you hear that, Mr. Bolan?"

"I heard it. Send her across."

"I ain't heard the deal yet."

"She's the first part. Look behind you. Look up, way up. Above the lagoon." . .

Harry was looking. So was everybody else around there. Then one of those damn whizzers came streaking across from nowhere and thundered into the hillside up there, way up there. When the smoke and settling earth cleared, that little waterfall had become a rushing torrent.

And the voice from heaven came down again: *"That's the second part. How much water, do you figure, is that dam holding back? How many more rockets, do you figure, will it take to let it all come down? And if it does come down—where do you figure you and your fifty boys will find to stand?"*

The answers to all that were too obvious to be denied. And there was a lot of moving around, a lot of uneasy voices making themselves heard in an unhappy chorus. Venturi turned back to the lake to mutter into it, "You're saying it's either this or that, eh?"

"That's what it is, yeah. Start the lady across. Then go and do what you've got to do. You send another canoe across in five minutes. Not six minutes. Five. If I like what I see, then—okay. You've got your deal."

"That's a hell of a deal, Mr. Bolan," Venturi complained.

"I know it is, Harry. I know it is. But it's the only deal I can consider. You do your part and you know I'll do mine. Right?"

Venturi sighed and scooped the little lady into his arms and carried her to the rack of canoes. He floated one, tossed in a paddle, and very tenderly placed the lady inside. "I could have a kid like you," he told her. "That's a hell of a guy you got up there. You treat 'im right."

Then he gave it a shove and watched until she was well underway.

A hell of a deal, yeah.

With one *hell* of a guy.

CHAPTER 19

MONDAY'S BOSSES

Bolan was at the con when she came inside, footsore and limping from the barefoot trek from the lakefront. She dropped beside him and wearily declared, "Didn't expect to ever see this place again, podner. Don't know how you worked that, soldier, but you have my undying—"

"You worked it yourself," he said softly. He did not look at her but continued scanning those quiet activities on the opposite shore. But he grinned and added, "Welcome home, warrior."

She said, "Just point me toward the liniment."

"Save it until we're clear," he suggested, "and I'll give you a navy shower."

"Could I hold you to that?"

"Sure. And don't underestimate the restorative powers of soap and water and loving hands."

She said, "Gosh, I can hardly wait. Uh, we're not clear yet?"

"Not really, no. I only had half a rearm for the rocket system. That means I have one bird left. And I suspect that dam up there could withstand quite a bit more than that."

"You were bluffing? What *is* that deal? What is it you were asking him to do?"

"For a guy like that—too much, maybe. Then again, maybe not. Harry's a survivor. He can reach down deep when he has to."

"You say that rather proudly."

He looked at her, then. "Harry's not as bad as some. The guy has a spark there, way down."

She dropped her eyes from that steady gaze and replied. "Yes, I . . . caught that, too. He was very sweet with me . . . almost fatherly. Told me to treat you right."

Bolan smiled. "You know what that means."

She smiled back. "Not what you're thinking, I bet. They found out about my . . . connections. I believe he was telling me to go easy on you."

Bolan chuckled and said, "Probably. What did you see over there?"

"Not much, I'm afraid. At first, I was too scared. Then I was too busy." She was fussing with the shirt, tucking the tails beneath her on the seat. "I must look like hell."

He said, "Not really, no. You look like a fed who just found her hard."

"Her what?" she asked, smiling quizzically.

"*Stay* hard, April," he told her, and turned back to his scans.

"Right now I'm feeling very soft," she said.

"There's a time for soft," he murmured.

"When will that time be?"

"Well . . . if the thing goes . . . we should be in Indy by nightfall."

"Meaning?"

"A time for soft," he said quietly.

"Not for you, bub," she replied naughtily.

He chuckled and let that one pass.

A moment later, he had the picture he'd been waiting for. He refined the focus and zoomed in for the close look. Then he sighed and told his lady, "There you go. He pulled it off. I wonder how many boys he had to walk on, to do it."

"What is it?" she asked, leaning toward the viewer.

It was Harry's part of the deal, yeah.

A canoe was gliding onto the lake.

It was unmanned.

Which is not to say that it was empty.

It held the heads of Monday's mob. Literally. Scarbo was there. Reina was there. Tuscanotte was there.

But not the whole men.

Just the heads.

EPILOGUE

They quietly withdrew the back way, gained the drive below the dam, and exited north onto Clay Lick Road. According to the navigator, they would intersect State Road 135 at Bean Blossom. That was a town, yeah, in this heartland of America.

Indianapolis, the Circle City, lay fifty minutes to the north. A C-135 aircraft awaited them there, to lift them away from the staggering remnants of Monday's Mob and into Terrible Tuesday.

During that airlift, the heavy cruiser would be refitted to help meet the challenges awaiting them at the end of that flight.

The man and woman would do some refitting, as well. Perhaps they would cement their new, as yet unspoken understanding. For sure they would bind each other's wounds and

177

strengthen the spiritual bonds already established by their walk through hell together.

For sure, neither would ever forget little Nashville and the breathless battle that had been fought there for human dignity and cosmic values.

The woman had her head on the man's shoulder—and she lifted it for a final look as they cleared that combat zone.

"Don't look back," he warned her. "Never look back."

"Why?" she asked.

"Just don't. It could lose your hard. Look straight ahead."

"I'm looking at *you*, soldier," she murmured.

And that, she knew, could lose her *heart*.